TRISTAN

SAN FRANCISCO SHOCKWAVES
BOOK 3

SAMANTHA LIND

SAMANTHALIND.COM

Tristan
San Francisco Shockwaves Book 3
Copyright 2023 Samantha Lind
All rights reserved.

Cover Design by JERSEY GIRL DESIGN
Cover image by WANDER AGUIAR
Cover Model THANE W.
Editing by Amy Briggs ~ Briggs Consulting LLC
Proofreading by Proof Before You Publish

❀ Created with Vellum

CONTENTS

1. Tristan   1
2. Kendra   10
3. Tristan   15
4. Kendra   25
5. Tristan   33
6. Kendra   39
7. Tristan   49
8. Kendra   58
9. Tristan   65
10. Kendra   74
11. Tristan   81
12. Kendra   93
13. Tristan   101
14. Kendra   116
15. Tristan   124
16. Kendra   140
17. Tristan   148
18. Kendra   156
19. Tristan   167
20. Kendra   184
21. Tristan   195
22. Kendra   203
23. Tristan   218
Epilogue   230

Coming Soon   237
Also by Samantha Lind   239
Acknowledgments   241
About the Author   243

CHAPTER 1
TRISTAN

THE SHRILL OF MY PHONE'S RINGER WAKES ME FROM A dead sleep. "Fucking hell, who's calling me at this hour?" I mutter to myself as I roll over, looking for the device. I roll directly into a warm and naked body. Memories from the night come flooding back to me. Just hours ago, I had a chick riding my face while another was riding my cock. The constant ringing forces me from my bed.

I stumble across my bedroom, searching for the obnoxiously loud device, finally finding it beneath the edge of my dresser.

"Hello," I groggily say into the phone.

"Tristan, where are you? I need help, man," my best friend, Jackson, says.

I slide a hand across my face; the amount of tequila I drank last night is not helping me much now. "I'm at home. What's up?"

"It's Kendra," he says, and my hackles instantly go up. Kendra is his little sister. I had to remind myself many times when we were teenagers that she was his little sister and not some chick I could lust after or fuck in the locker room at school.

"What about Kendra?" I bite out as bile from all the alcohol last night burns the back of my throat.

"She needs help, and I don't know what to do," he cries into the phone.

"What about Kendra? What happened?" I repeat. My words are more biting than before.

"I don't know yet; she's being checked out by a doctor now. He really did a number on her. I'm going to fucking kill him," Jackson trails off.

"Doctor?" I question. "I'll kill the motherfucker that touched her," I seethe.

"He did a number on her," Jackson's voice cracks again. "We need to get her away from him once and for all."

"She can come here," I tell him.

"Are you sure?" he asks. "She's going to need some help; can you give her that?"

"I can get whatever help she might need."

"It's bad, Tristan." I can hear the desperation in his voice.

"I'll try to be there by the end of the day. What hospital are you at?" I ask, already making a mental note of what I must do to fly home and bring back my best friend's little sister.

"We're at Mass General; I'll text you if she's discharged before you arrive."

"Sounds good. I'll text you my flight info once I can get something booked."

"Thanks, man. I appreciate it." He sounds slightly relieved, which makes me feel better.

"Of course, you know I love Kendra like a sister. I'd do anything for her," I say, reminding myself more than him that I need to think of her as my sister, not a woman who can warm my bed.

"I gotta go; a nurse is flagging me down."

"Text me an update on her condition," I tell him before the line goes dead.

I blow out a deep breath and close my eyes. I say a little prayer that Kendra is okay, or, at least, she will be. She's been dating the asshole of all assholes for the last four years. One that I'd like to introduce to my fist a few hundred times over. Let him know what it's like to go up against someone his own size, not a woman half that.

Guys that hit women are the lowest of scum in my book.

Jackson has tried to convince Kendra to leave Chad, but she's never stayed away. He's always slimed his way back into her good graces, only to fuck up again within a few months. Hopefully, if she agrees to come back to California with me, it will give her the distance she needs to leave him in her past where he belongs.

I turn back toward my bed, finding one of the chicks sitting up and looking at me like I'm crazy for being up and on the phone at this hour. "Come back to bed; let me suck on that cock again," she says, trying to be sexy.

"Sorry, sweetheart, I've got to go, so that means you've got to go," I tell her, my voice stern. "Your friend, as well," I add, nodding toward the other sleeping form in my bed.

She obviously doesn't like my brush-off, if the frown is telling. "But I'm ready for another round," she says, spreading her legs, trying to entice me with her naked body.

"I said it was time to go," I practically growl. "I don't have time for your shit; I just need you gone." I raise my voice so she knows I'm serious and won't give in to her antics.

"What's all the yelling for?" the second girl asks as she sits up and pushes her hair out of her face. She blinks a few times, getting her bearings about her as she looks between me, standing across the room, and her friend, who is naked and sprawled on the bed.

I can tell the tequila did a number on her, as it did me, by how she holds the side of her head like the room is spinning on a tilt-a-whirl. "I just got an emergency call, and I need to go; therefore, the two of you need to go," I tell her before her friend can interject. "I was just explaining this to your friend; she wasn't too happy."

My words must snap her out of her sleepy and drunk haze as she jumps out of bed and starts grabbing clothes off the floor, pulling some on, and tossing others on the bed for her friend. "I hope everything is okay, we'll get out of your way," she says once fully dressed.

"Thank you," I say as I run a hand over my face. I need a tall glass of water, and some ibuprofen for what I'm sure will be a killer headache.

I go in search of just that as they collect the rest of their things, and the blonde one finishes getting dressed. I can hear them talking from where I'm downing water and meds from the master bathroom. "We'll let ourselves out; hope everything is okay," the second chick calls out. I grab a towel from a hook, wrap it around my waist, and then follow them out of my bedroom.

"Sorry about the middle of the night interruption, but I've just got to take care of things. Please be safe getting home," I tell them. I look around to see if I can find my wallet. I'm not an asshole, and I want them to make it home safely.

"We're good," the second chick says. "I've already got an Uber ordered; it should be here in less than five minutes."

"Okay," I tell them as they walk out my door. I shut it quietly as they walk away, my body falling against it as the adrenaline from Jackson's call comes crashing down.

I drag my tired and hungover body to the shower. I need to find a flight, pack a bag, and get my ass to the airport, but I can't do any of that without something helping to wake me up.

I let the hot water rain over me for a few minutes. The water feels good on my tired body. Once out, I dry off and wrap my towel back around my waist before I brush my teeth. The alcohol breath is already making me regret the amount of tequila I drank last night.

I pull on some joggers and a Henley. Both will be comfortable traveling on a cross-country flight today. I head into the kitchen and flip on the coffee pot. I'm going to need some caffeine to get through the day.

While the coffee brews, I start searching for a flight back to Boston. I check the time, it's just now four am on the dot. A flight leaving at seven gets me there by mid-to-late afternoon. It will be tight, but I can be at the airport in time to make the flight, so I quickly book it.

With a cup of coffee poured, I head back into my bedroom and pull out my carry-on bag. I've been packing for road trips now for years; I'm a pro at it. I grab my fully stocked toiletry bag, toss in a few changes of clothes, and zip it up. I grab a backpack and add my charging cords, iPad, and noise canceling headphones. Hopefully, I'll get lucky and grab a five-hour nap on the flight.

I easily make it to the airport, my Uber dropping me off at an entrance not far from the security checkpoint, which I quickly make my way through. Got to love pre-check as I sail right past the line that is starting to form.

The restaurants and fast-food places are all busy grilling breakfast for the tired passengers. The smell of the greasy food hits my nose, and my stomach starts grumbling, reminding me, once again, I drank way too much tequila just a few hours ago. I check the time on my phone and am shocked when I realize just how few hours have passed since I was partying it up. I shake out of my haze and go in search of some food and water to hold me over until I get to Boston.

"Hey, handsome," a sultry voice says from next to me as I wait for my order.

I look up from my phone, locking eyes with the woman. She's pretty, but not my type. I give her a polite smile but do my best not to engage.

"You look so familiar; do I know you from some-where?" she asks.

"Not that I'm aware," I tell her. "But I get that a lot, people like to say I've got one of those faces."

"I swear I've seen you or met you somewhere," she insists.

"Holy shit, you're Tristan Henderson," some guy says, stopping to point at me.

"Shit," I mutter just as my name is called by the barista. I step up to the counter and thank her as I grab my order.

"Hey, man." I greet the guy who obviously knows who I am. It doesn't surprise me, since my face is plas-tered all over the place thanks to the Shockwaves marketing department. All of us are, they like using our faces to promote the team. "Are you a fan?" I ask him.

"Sure am. I was so excited when they announced hockey was coming to the Bay Area."

"We're sure glad to be here, so thanks for the support. Can I sign something for you quickly, or take a picture? I don't mean to rush, but I've got a flight to catch," I tell him. The woman who was trying to talk to me as I waited has lost interest, thank god.

"That would be amazing, thank you," he says as he stands next to me and pulls out his phone. He holds it up and snaps a couple selfies before he's satisfied with them.

"Have a good day, I've got to jet," I say as I start to push my bag and head toward my gate.

I make it with only a few minutes to spare before

they start boarding, so perfect timing to scarf down my breakfast sandwich while I wait.

> Flight lands around 3:30, I'll let you know when I get there. Any news?

The text sends, but sits as delivered for what feels like forever until it switches to read, and the three little bubbles start dancing as Jackson starts typing back to me.

> They just let me in to see her. She's got a few broken ribs, some stitches on her cheek, and a broken wrist. Otherwise, she's fine. No internal injuries.

> Fuck. Is she awake and talking to you?

> Sleeping right now, it's been a traumatic night, so they said to let her sleep. They gave her a good dose of pain meds, which they said would help her sleep. They can't take all the pain away, but they can at least help with it.

> Those ribs are going to be the worst. I've cracked enough in my life to know firsthand what that's like. They just called for boarding, so I'll talk to you when I'm on the ground.

> Love ya, brother. Thanks for coming.

> You know it. Anything for family.

I walk up to the gate, pulling up my boarding pass on my phone to scan at the desk before walking down the jetway. I get settled into my first-class window seat. I was lucky they had one available; the cost was well worth it for the long flight.

"Good morning, and welcome aboard. I'm Tori, and I'll be the flight attendant in first class today. Can I get you anything while you settle in this morning?" Tori asks.

"I'm good for now; I hope to sleep most of the way," I tell her honestly.

"Of course, don't hesitate to flag me down if you need something."

"Thanks, Tori," I tell her as I flash her a smile. I don't miss the way her ears and neck start to redden with a blush. She quickly turns to the next row, introducing herself and offering to get them something.

I settle into my seat, pulling out my headphones and iPad. I get some music playing, wrap my travel pillow around my neck and get as comfortable as I possibly can for the long flight.

CHAPTER 2
KENDRA

AN INSISTENT BEEPING BRINGS ME OUT OF THE FOG I FEEL like I'm in. I can't see anything, but I can definitely feel the pain. My entire body is throbbing as I attempt to suck in a deep breath. The memories flood my mind, the hits to my body, the intense pain I felt as I wished I'd die just so the pain would end.

"Kendra." I can hear a familiar voice call my name as it cracks. I recognize it but can't think straight enough to figure out who it is. "Kendra," he says again, and more tears fall from my eyes. I can feel them as they roll down my cheeks.

"Jackson?" I croak out, my voice raspy and whisper-soft from my grogginess.

"I'm right here," he assures me as he gently encloses my hand in his own. I blink a few times, only seeing him out of one of my eyes; the other feels heavy and swollen and unable to open.

"Where are we?" I ask him.

"Mass General, we've been here for a few hours

already. I've never been so scared," he starts to say, his voice cracking as he lifts my hand to his lips and kisses it.

"I'm sorry," I croak out.

"You don't have anything to be sorry about. That motherfucker will pay for what he did to you," Jackson seethes.

"I can't go back, he'll kill me," I cry.

"There will be no going back. I already called Tristan. He's coming here to help. He said you can go with him."

"I don't think that's a good idea," I start to protest.

"Please just think about it. Even if it's just for a little while."

I can feel more tears burning the back of my eyelids. The last person on earth I want to see me like this is Tristan.

"You're awake," a nurse says as she enters the room and takes me in. I watch out of my one eye as she rubs sanitizer all over her hands as she approaches the side of my hospital bed. "How are you feeling?"

"Like I was run over by a bus."

"I'll check to see if you can have another dose of pain meds. Can you tell me where your pain is on a scale of one to ten, ten being the worst pain?"

"A nine," I say, hoping like hell I can have some more pain meds. "Can you tell me what is wrong; what my injuries are?" I ask as she leans over me to listen to my heart and lungs.

"I've paged the doctor; he'll want to talk to you now that you're awake. He'll also go over everything with you. It shouldn't be too much longer, as he wanted to be notified as soon as you woke back up."

"Thank you, it hurts so bad to take a deep breath," I tell her as she moves the stethoscope to a new spot to listen to me.

"That's probably the broken ribs you have. They'll be sore for at least a couple of weeks."

"Broken ribs?" I question.

"Yes, honey, you have four of them. I'll get you another pillow, hold on to them, it can help with the pain some," she tells me as she opens a cabinet in the corner and pulls out a pillow, then slips it into a pillowcase before placing it next to me on the bed.

My attention is pulled toward the door as a man in scrubs walks in. He looks young for a doctor, but what the hell do I know. I'm a twenty-four-year-old fucked up girl with nothing to show for my life.

"Ms. Torres, I'm Dr. Cotter. I'm glad to see you awake, you've suffered a lot in the past twenty-four hours or so. Can you tell me how your pain is?" he asks as he stands next to my hospital bed.

"Bad, a nine. It hurts to breathe, my entire body hurts," I tell him as more tears form, burning my eyes.

Dr. Cotter turns to the nurse; I still don't know her name. "When was the last dose of pain meds?" he asks.

"Just under four hours ago," she tells him as she checks the computer screen in front of her.

"Sounds like you're in luck, we can get you another dose of some meds. They might help you rest, which you need a lot of to get out of here."

"I know about the ribs, but can you tell me what else

he did?" I ask. Tears stream down my face as I lose control of holding them back.

"Are you okay with me discussing personal things with those in the room?" he asks. Jackson is the only one in here besides the doctor and nurse. I can't imagine what they could want to protect my brother from knowing about me.

"That's fine," I tell him. "You can list my brother as an approved person on my chart."

"I'll get that noted," the nurse says as she types away at the computer.

"The big things, you have four broken ribs. They will take weeks, possibly months to fully heal. The worst of the pain will be in the first few weeks, then gradually get better. Your facial x-rays showed a broken eye socket," he says, and I gasp, reaching up to touch my swollen eye. "I had orthopedics consult on it, and they cleared you from needing surgery. Keeping it iced is the best thing you can do for it. You have multiple smaller cuts and bruising covering about half of your body. We ran blood and urine tests, along with ultrasounds and a few x-rays. We believe you were drugged, but amazingly enough, even after all of the trauma you survived, so did your baby."

The room gets eerily quiet. Did he just say baby? My head is spinning with everything he just told me I suffered through, clearly, I heard him wrong.

"You're pregnant?" Jackson asks, breaking the silence.

I turn my head so I can look at him out of my one

good eye. He must realize I'm just as shocked as he is at this news.

"I take it that is news to you?" Dr. Cotter asks.

"Yes, how far along?" I ask, my mind already racing with how in the hell will I raise a child. I can hardly take care of myself.

"The ultrasound put you at about seven weeks. Do you have an OBGYN?"

"Yeah, well, at least one that I've seen a few times for my yearly appointment and birth control."

"We can call their office and have the doctor come check on you and the baby, or I can call OB here for one, but I'd like for you to be checked out by someone else just to make sure we didn't miss anything."

"Okay," I agree with him. My mind is racing on how I keep this from Chad. If he was to find out about this baby, he'd hold it over my head for the rest of my life, and I'll never be rid of him.

"You have options," Jackson pipes up. He must be able to read my mind as I lay here completely shell-shocked.

"He's right, you do have options, if you need someone to come in and talk over those with you, I'm happy to arrange for that. I understand that you're in a bad position right now and this news might not be what you were expecting."

"Thank you, I'll think about it and let you know," I tell him as sleep threatens to pull me under again. The pain meds must be kicking in, as all of a sudden, I can't fight the pull and my eyes close.

CHAPTER 3
TRISTAN

I GRAB MY SUITCASE FROM THE OVERHEAD BAGGAGE compartment before exiting the plane and heading straight for the exit. I pull out my phone, ordering a ride to take me straight to the hospital. I texted Jackson as soon as the wheels touched the tarmac, and I was able to take my phone off airplane mode. I would have texted him throughout the flight, but I passed out for the majority of it.

"Hello," the driver greets me as I slide into the back seat of the SUV. She's a cheery older lady, reminding me of my grandmother.

"Afternoon, ma'am," I greet her back.

"Just to confirm, it looks like we're headed to the hospital," she asks, looking at me in her rearview mirror.

"That's correct, the main entrance is fine."

"Of course." She pulls out of the pick-up area and maneuvers through the airport traffic. This a busy airport, so there is a lot of traffic, especially at this time of day. "Can't be a good thing if you're headed straight to the hospital from the airport," she states.

"Not really, just a family friend who needs some support." I find myself confiding in her. I rub a hand down my tired face, wiping my eyes. My hangover is long gone, but I still feel the effects of all the alcohol I consumed last night.

"Lucky to have you, it sounds," she muses.

"Sometimes family is who you choose, not who shares your blood. I'd do anything for them."

"I completely agree," she muses "Is Boston where you're originally from?"

"Yes, ma'am. Grew up not far from here, but now I call California home."

"Ah, traded in the cold for the warmth, I see." She flashes a quick smile over her shoulder.

"Something like that, although, I somehow find myself in the cold there often."

"You can take the boy out of the cold, but you can't take the cold out of the boy, I suppose."

I just chuckle at her analogy. I've heard that many times before.

Our easy chit-chat comes to an end when she pulls up to the main entrance of the hospital. I open my door and grab my suitcase and backpack before exiting the SUV. "Thank you for the ride and conversation, have a great rest of your day," I say.

"Here's my card, if you find yourself needing any more rides, feel free to text me and I'll let you know if I'm out and about."

"Thank you, I appreciate that." I tuck the card she

holds out into my pocket. I'm not sure if I'll need many rides, but it was nice to get a friendly person who didn't gush over who I am and what I do for a living.

I enter the hospital and find the elevator bank. Jackson already gave me the room information and what tower I'd find them in. I grab a coffee and sandwich from the coffee shop near the elevators before getting on and heading up to find Kendra's room.

Jackson warned me she's pretty battered and bruised, so I'm prepared for the worst. I knock my knuckles on the cracked open door, waiting to hear if it's okay for me to enter. The door swings open, and my best friend is standing on the other side. He looks like shit. Like he's aged a decade since I last saw him, which was only a few weeks ago. He steps out of the room, pulling me into a bear hug. I hold him tight and can feel the stress roll off of him.

"Can I see her?" I ask him as we stand outside the hospital room.

"Yeah, the doctor was in just a little bit ago. They gave her another dose of pain meds and they've made her fall back to sleep. I'm just warning you; she's pretty roughed up."

"Any word on the asshole being arrested yet?" I ask as Jackson turns and pushes the door open. There is a curtain blocking the view into the room for privacy, I'm sure. We step around it and the air leaves my lungs when I first take her in. She looks so small in the large hospital bed, covered with blankets, and surrounded by a few pillows. I can see the bruised and swollen eye, along with some other small cuts and bruises on her face. The asshole better hope I never see him.

"Fuck," I mumble as I step closer, running my fingertips lightly over the top of her hand. Her skin is warm under my touch and sends shockwaves up my arm.

"It's going to be a long road, both physically and mentally," Jackson says quietly as he stands beside me.

"Has the doctor said how long they think she'll be here?" I ask.

"Not really. I think they're still trying to get her pain under control."

Jackson and I take a seat on the small sofa and start talking about my upcoming season. I can tell he needs a distraction and to not talk about Kendra right now. My mind is also running with how I'm going to help her. My schedule doesn't really have me home every night and I'm not sure if she'd want to be in a strange new city all alone for multiple days at a time. I'm starting to think my offer was too much. Maybe I can offer to pay for a place for her to live here if she doesn't want to come back to California with me.

"Jackson," a groggy voice calls from the other side of the room. He is on his feet in a matter of seconds and by Kendra's side.

"I'm right here," he tells her as he holds her hand. "Tristan is also here," he says as he motions for me to join him next to her bed. I walk over, standing on the opposite side as Jackson is.

"Hi," she says to me as I take her in once again.

"Hi, sweetheart, how's your pain?" I ask.

"Excruciating," she says. I find myself reaching for the call button to alert the nurse. There's got to be something they can do to help her more.

"This is the nurses' station, how can I help you?" a voice comes over the speaker.

"Kendra is awake again and her pain is bad, is there anything she can be given to help?" I say.

"I'll send her nurse in shortly to check on her," the nurse says.

"Thank you," Kendra answers for us. "How was your flight?" she asks me.

"Uneventful. I'm pretty sure I fell asleep before they even finished boarding and woke up as we started to descend. Then, I came straight here from the airport," I tell her as I motion to my suitcase and backpack sitting in the corner.

"Thank you," she whispers. A tear rolls down her cheek and I find myself reaching out to swipe it away. The moment my fingers graze her skin, she flinches, and I want to kick my own ass.

"I'm sorry, did I hurt you?" I ask as I quickly pull my hand away from her.

"Just tender on that cheek," she says as her hand finds mine.

We're interrupted when the door opens and a nurse walks in. "Hi Kendra, I'm Wanda, your new nurse for the night. How are you doing?" the older woman asks as she starts to assess Kendra.

"My pain is back at level nine," she tells her. Both Jackson and I step back away from the hospital bed, giving the nurse room to do her job.

"I'm sorry, sweetie, let me check your orders and see what I can do to fix that. Have you tried eating anything yet?"

"No, not yet."

"She hasn't been brought anything other than ice chips and water, do I need to go out and get her something?" Jackson asks Wanda.

"Oh no, I'll get a dinner tray ordered. Let me see if I can find the menu and you can pick what you'd like."

"Thank you, that'd be great," Jackson says.

Wanda finishes taking Kendra's vitals, then taps away at the computer near the bed. "It looks like Dr. Cotter has approved a new pain medication, one that hopefully will last longer, but also not make you as sleepy."

"That sounds divine," Kendra tells her.

"I'll be right back; I need to go get it from the med station."

Wanda steps out of the room and Kendra turns her head our way. "The two of you can head out for the night, if you'd like. It isn't like I'm going anywhere."

"Not going anywhere," Jackson tells her. "This is right where I need to be."

"I'm good for now."

"All right, here is a menu for you to pick from, and I'll get this pain med going," Wanda says as she waltzes back into the room. She has a calmness about her when she enters the room. "You should start to feel some relief in just another minute or so. This is the good stuff and don't worry, it is safe for the baby."

I swear I heard her wrong, did she just say baby? I

quickly look to Jackson, who must notice my quick jerky movements as his eyes find mine. A slight nod of his head tells me I heard the nurse correctly. Kendra's pregnant with that asshole's baby. *Fuck.*

I wait for Wanda to finish up with Kendra, she promises her dinner tray will arrive shortly so that she isn't starving for much longer.

"Thank you," Kendra tells her as she leaves the room. "I just found out a few hours ago," she says as she turns our way in the bed. "I had no idea; it wasn't like I was trying to get pregnant. The doctor said I'm about seven weeks."

"Is everything okay with the baby?" I ask, not sure how to tread as I can't get a good read on what she thinks of the news.

"So far. The doctor wanted me to be checked out by an OBGYN just to verify, but that hasn't happened yet."

"Probably for the best." I trail off when a knock at the door pulls our attention away.

"Hello, Miss Torres, I'm Dr. Kane, I'm one of the OBGYN residents here in the hospital. I was sent for a consult; do you mind if I come in and do that now?"

"That's fine," she tells the young woman.

"Hello." The doctor gives Jackson and me a quick smile and wave of her hand. "Do the two of you mind stepping out of the room for a few minutes while I perform the exam?" she asks us. My hackles go up, but then, I realize this is what Kendra needs.

"Of course," Jackson tells her. "Do you need anything, sis?" he asks Kendra.

"I'm good," she assures him, then her eye finds

mine. I can tell she's trying to say something in that look, I just can't quite figure it out.

We step outside just as Wanda heads into the room with a tray of food. I'm sure she'll be happy to have that once the exam is done.

"I need some food, want to head down to the cafeteria while we wait?" Jackson asks.

"Sure. I scarfed down a sandwich when I got here, but I could eat something else," I tell him as we head down the long hall toward the elevator bank. We're quiet on the ride down to the lower level where the cafeteria is located. I don't spend much time in hospitals, so I'm quite surprised at how large it is and how much they offer for food options. We both load up a tray with food, stopping quickly at the cashier to pay before we find a table to sit down at and chow down.

"I can't thank you enough for getting here so quickly. I about lost my shit when I got the call she'd been brought in by ambulance."

"Of course, you're family to me."

"I don't know how to help her once she's out of here, man," he breaks down.

"The offer still stands; she can come back to California with me. It might be an adjustment for both of us, but we can make it work. My place has a second bedroom with its own private bathroom, plus, the large living room and kitchen I hardly ever use, other than to reheat meals I order in."

"She's going to need medical care, and probably a shit ton of counseling after what that asshole put her through."

"I'm sure I can get some referrals from the team doctors or my teammates with significant others." I pull my cell out and tap on my captain, Ryker's, contact and type out a text message.

> Hey man, I've had a family emergency and had to fly back home this morning. I might be coming back with my best friend's sister, but she's going to need some support. Can Avery maybe help me out if she comes back with me?

The message is read immediately, and the bubbles pop up almost instantly.

> She says anything she can do to help, just let her know. Keep us updated on when you'll be back, and we can get everyone rounded up to welcome her to the fold.

> Thanks man, I'll let you know. Things are still a little unknown at the moment. At the hospital waiting for more information about when she'll be released.

> Fuck man, I hope everything is okay.

> Let's just say her ex better hope I never find him.

> Just don't get yourself thrown in jail.
> You can't help her from behind bars.

I show Jackson my messages with Ryker before I

tuck my phone back in my pocket and go back to eating.

"Sounds like a good guy, you still enjoying it out there?" he asks.

"I do. It's one of the best teams I've been on. I was a little nervous when I got picked up in the expansion draft, but it was one of those things that I didn't know I needed until it happened. Hopefully, this season will be even better now that we've got a season under us. We've started to create that chemistry needed on the ice. Friendships have been made and we're really gelling as a team."

"That's great to hear. I miss getting to see you play all the time."

"You'll have to make a trip out this season, catch a few home games."

"Yeah, maybe," he half-ass commits. I'm sure if Kendra ends up out in California with me, he'll end up coming out to see both of us.

We finish up our food and take our trays to the drop station before we head back upstairs. I can't imagine the doctor is still in with Kendra for the exam, at this point, unless something is wrong. That thought has me picking up my pace as we make our way back to her room.

CHAPTER 4
KENDRA

"Everything is looking good, no signs of bleeding or trauma to the baby," Dr. Kane tells me as she removes her exam gloves. I'm so thankful they sent a female doctor. I'm not sure I would have survived the internal exam with a male doctor right now.

"Do you know what my options are?" I ask her timidly.

She gives me a tender smile and takes a seat on the edge of my bed. "I read your chart before coming in to see you. You've been through hell. You absolutely have options right now. At seven weeks, you can still choose to terminate the pregnancy. If that isn't something you want, there is always adoption or keeping and raising the baby yourself. I know this is all probably very overwhelming, but only you can decide what is the right option for you. If you want to think about everything, you have time to do that."

My tears run freely down my face; at this point, I've stopped even trying to keep them back. "I never thought I'd be in this situation," I tell her honestly. "I knew I needed to get out, I just didn't know how. When I tried, this is where it landed me," I confide in the doctor.

"There are resources available to you. Have you talked to one of the hospital's social workers yet?" she asks.

"No, I've been mostly out of it today. The pain meds they had me on kept knocking me out."

"Understandable. Now that you've been switched to a new one, you should be able to stay awake more. I can put in a request for one of them to come up and see you tomorrow, if you'd like."

"Sure, that'd be great. I'm probably going to need help finding a safe place to live once I'm discharged. I can only sleep on my brother's couch for so many nights before I'll go crazy."

"Are your parents anywhere nearby?" she asks.

"They live about an hour away, and it's a possibility, but our relationship is also a little strained. They weren't a fan of my ex."

"Do they know that you are in the hospital?"

"I don't know. I have my brother listed as my emergency contact," I tell her. "I don't have my phone, so I haven't contacted anyone, and my brother hasn't told me if he's contacted them yet."

"You have time to figure things out, and it sounds like you have the support of your brother."

"He's a good one, so is his best friend. He dropped everything to get on a flight to come here this morning," I tell her. "I'm pretty sure I remember my brother telling me Tristan said I could go back to California with him if I wanted to."

"I take it those were the two men in here when I arrived?"

"Yeah. My brother is the one with the beard, and his friend is the tatted-up one. He's a professional hockey player."

"You're a lucky girl to have them in your corner." She flashes me a quick smile.

"Yeah, I suppose. Now, to just not royally fuck my life up like I have so far. I have so many good men in my life, yet I can't seem to pick a good one when it comes to the guys I date."

"Honey, I get it. It sometimes takes kissing a hell of a lot of frogs before you find your prince, but I have faith you will one day look back at this time in your life and realize how strong you are from it all."

"I can only hope. Maybe a new start in California is what I need," I state, hoping that I'm remembering what Jackson said Tristan offered earlier today.

"A new start is never a bad thing, definitely something to explore and see if it's what you want. The most important thing is for you to do what's right for you and will keep you safe," Dr. Kane says as she looks down at a pager device that is vibrating. She stands up quickly and tucked her items back into her pockets. "Sorry to cut our conversation short, but I'm needed in labor and delivery."

"Thank you for talking to me, today has been a little overwhelming and my brother has been hovering over me all day."

"It shows he cares," she says. "And of course, I'll leave you my card, if you have any questions, feel free to call or text me."

"Thanks, and good luck."

I watch as Dr. Kane drops a business card on the counter before she steps out of my room. For the first time since I've been awake, I'm alone. The silence is welcoming, yet also reminds me just how alone I am. Yes, I have Jackson here to help me, and he's been great, but how long can he really stay by my side helping me? Then, there's Tristan. Is his offer real? Could I see myself moving out to California, where the only person I know is the man I've crushed on the entire time I've known him? The man who should probably be off limits to me, since he is my brother's best friend, and all.

I relax into the bed, my eyes closing as I think about what my life is going to look like moving forward.

The door opens abruptly, causing me to startle and jump slightly in my bed. The searing pain shooting through my body from the sudden movement has me crying out in pain.

"Shit, are you okay?" Jackson asks, coming to my side.

"Yeah," I grit out. "I'll be fine," I tell him as tears, once again, burn the back of my eyes.

"Nurses' station, how can I help you?" I hear a voice say.

"She's in intense pain, can she have anything?" Jackson asks.

"I'll send in the nurse," the woman says.

"Thanks," he tells her before the call drops. "Do you

want help sitting up more or maybe lying further down?" he asks me. His hand gently smooths over the top of my head, brushing my hair off of my forehead.

"I'll be fine, just need to sit still and the pain will subside," I tell him as I blow out a breath and tug the pillow a little tighter. The sharp pains are already subsiding as I do just as I tell him.

Wanda enters the room, and I notice she doesn't close the door completely behind her, which she's never done. "How are you doing? I got a call that you were in excruciating pain."

"I think she'd drifted off to sleep and when we came back from dinner the door opening scared her, so she flinched and is now suffering because of that," Jackson tells her.

"Sudden movements will definitely aggravate things. Unfortunately, it's too soon to give you anything additional for the pain. We can try a different position to see if that will help," Wanda offers.

"I'll be fine, it is already subsiding," I tell her.

"All right, there are two police officers here that would like to get your statement. Do you feel up to talking to them?" she asks in her sweet grandmotherly way.

"I guess," I tell her. I didn't realize that I'd have to talk to anyone about what I experienced, but maybe that means that he'll actually be held accountable for his actions.

"I'll let them know they can come on in." Wanda gives my hand a little squeeze and I can tell it's a *you've got this* type of squeeze.

She exits the room and a few seconds later two women enter the room, both dressed in business attire. "Ms. Torres, I'm Detective Brown and this is my partner, Detective Robs. Is now a good time for you to answer a few questions and for us to get your victim statement?" Detective Brown greets.

"Now's fine, not like I've got anywhere better to be." I try and crack a joke to lighten it up in here just a little bit, but no one caves to my attempts.

"Can you walk us through what you remember from last night?" the other detective, I think her name was Robs, asks.

I suck in a breath, wincing when I momentarily forget about my pain. I don't know some of the details, as I was out of it, but I recount everything that I can remember, all while the two detectives take notes. If they missed anything, they also recorded everything I told them for their report.

"Thank you for your time, if we need anything else, we'll be in touch. Do you have a safe place to go once you're released?" Detective Brown asks.

"We'll be keeping her safe," Jackson answers for me.

"Is she allowed to leave the state?" Tristan asks. "I've offered to take her back to California with me, if she so chooses."

"Kendra can go wherever she feels the safest. If we need anything, we'll reach out," Detective Robs tells him, turning back in my direction. "If things go to trial, you would be needed as the key witness, however, that will be months down the road."

"Do you think it will come to that?" I ask, not loving

the idea that I'd have to sit on the witness stand and recount everything I lived through.

"There's no telling. We have a significant amount of evidence, but it is up to the DA's office if they'll offer a plea deal, then he'd have to accept the plea."

"We'll be here to support you through whatever happens," Jackson tells me as he comes to stand near my head.

"Thank you," I tell him.

"If you think of anything else, even if it is a minor thing, you call one of us and we can add it to our records in the case."

"Will do, thank you," I tell them again. As overwhelming as it was to give my statement, I'm just glad that it is over. It's lifted an invisible weight off of my chest I didn't even realize was there.

THE LAST TWO DAYS HAVE BEEN A WHIRLWIND, BUT I'M finally being discharged from the hospital. I got word from the two detectives that came and took my statement, Chad is in custody and is awaiting his first arraignment.

"You take care of yourself, and you accept all the help that you're offered," Wanda tells me as she hugs me.

"Thank you, and I will. I don't ever want to be back in this situation ever."

"That's what I like to hear." I take the folder she holds out to me that contains all my discharge paperwork, along with my prescriptions for the next few days.

"All ready?" Jackson asks as he walks back into my room. "Tristan is waiting in the car at the front doors."

"In the wheelchair you go," Wanda instructs.

"I can walk," I tell her.

"It's hospital policy, so in you go," she says, and I don't fight her on it. I take a seat, holding the pillow to my torso to help with my ribs.

The ride down to the first floor is quick, and as Jackson said, Tristan is parked right outside the door in Jackson's SUV, waiting for us.

"Do you want to sit in the front or back?" Jackson asks as we stop next to the SUV.

"I'm not picky," I tell him as Wanda leans down to move the footrests out of the way.

"Upfront it is," Jackson says as he opens the door, then turns to help me stand up and shuffle into the vehicle. He helps me get settled with the seatbelt secured, then hands me my pillow to hold once again.

"Take good care of her," I hear Wanda tell him as my door closes.

I can't hear his reply, but I can only imagine what he told her. She steps back with the wheelchair and gives me a quick wave before turning and disappearing back into the hospital. Jackson slides into the backseat, settling in as Tristan pulls out and into traffic.

CHAPTER 5
TRISTAN

I set the weights back on the rack, then swipe the sweat from my forehead. It feels good to get a full workout in after the last few days of sitting around the hospital until the nurses would kick us out at night.

"Please tell me we're done," Jackson wheezes from where he's sprawled out on the floor.

Chuckling, I toss my sweaty towel perfectly, so it smacks him in the face. "Don't tell me you're tired, we've got another set to go yet," I tease.

"Fuck that, I'm not sure how I'm going to move after all that."

"I'm just fucking with you, we're done," I tell him as I offer him a hand and help pull him up to stand.

"I needed that, especially after the past few days."

"Same, bro, same."

We head for the locker room, both taking our time as we shower off the sweat before heading out.

"I'm starving, let's pick up some lunch before

heading back to your place," I suggest to Jackson as we walk out to his SUV.

"Sounds like a plan. Want to shoot Kendra a text to see if she'd like anything?" he asks as he slides into the driver's seat.

> We're stopping to grab lunch; can we bring anything back for you?

> Yes please, let me know where you stop, and I'll pick something.

> We can stop wherever you'd like, what are you craving?

> I'm not picky, wherever you go I'll be good with.

> I know you're not picky, still doesn't mean you can't pick what you want.

I can tell she's so used to not being given a choice, and that pisses me right the fuck off. Just another reason I'd like to find the asswipe she was dating and show him a thing or two about how you treat a woman.

> I'm not picky Tristan. But to appease you, the half sandwich half soup combo from Panera would be amazing.

I smile as I read her text.

> See was that so hard?

> Terrible {rolling eye emoji}

> I knew you could do it, now what kind of sandwich and soup?

> Grilled cheese and tomato soup

> Anything to drink?

> I'm good, but thanks.

"She'd like a soup and sandwich combo from Panera," I relay to Jackson, "so we can either grab something for ourselves there, as well, or grab it after we get our food," I tell him.

"I'm fine with whatever," he says. "There's one just up the road from here."

"Sounds good to me," I tell him as he pulls out of the gym's parking lot and heads for the restaurant.

We arrive just at the perfect time, as the line is nonexistent, but by the time we finish ordering it is all the way to the door.

"Did you order everything on the menu?" Kendra asks as we set all the bags down on the counter.

"I was starving, so we ordered a few different options. Don't worry, we won't let any of it go to waste." I wink at her as I start to unpack the bags. I find her order and hand it over.

"How are you feeling, do you need any pain meds or anything at all?" Jackson asks Kendra after we've all finished eating. She's settled in on his recliner, and for the first time since I arrived, actually looks comfortable. It seemed like the only color she had was the bruising, but now that she isn't in the hospital, she's starting to look a little more human. The swelling of her eye has gone down a lot, enough so that she can actually open it now and see out of it. Thankfully, the broken eye socket didn't do any permanent damage to her eyesight.

"I'm good," she tells him, a little bit of frustration evident in her voice. "You don't have to baby me, I'm a big girl and can ask for help when I need it," she sasses.

"I know, and I'm sorry if I'm hovering. I just can't get the image out of my mind when I first saw you in the ER the other night," he tells her somberly.

"I'm sorry for snapping at you. I know you're just trying to help, and I can't express enough how much I appreciate it. I love you," she tells him. "And thank you, Tristan, for flying all the way out here to be Jackson's support. I know he needed you."

"You know I consider both of you family," I tell her. "And my offer still stands, if you want to get out of here. Be it a week, a month, or a permanent move, my guest bedroom is yours for the taking. I even have some friends ready to help you settle in if you come back with me."

"Aren't you gone a lot?" she asks.

"Half of my season is played on the road. Sometimes that puts me on the road for just a night or two, but we'll occasionally have a ten-day road trip. I think most average three to four days."

"Can I think about it?" she asks, and I can tell she's unsure about the offer, if the way she worries her bottom lip between her teeth is any indication.

"Of course. You can even come out after I head back, if that's what you decide."

"When do you have to head back?" she asks.

"I need to fly back no later than Sunday as I have to report to the rink on Monday for the start of training camp."

"I figured it would be soon." She picks at the fizzy blanket draped over her lap.

"I'm not sure how I'd pay for a ticket out there. I don't have a job and I'm sure Chad cut off my card before he was arrested."

"Don't worry about the ticket, if you want to come out, I'll buy it for you. Just like I won't charge you rent, and my kitchen comes well stocked," I tell her, attempting to take away any levels of stress that I can.

"I-I don't know what to say," she says tearfully. I stand up and close the distance between the couch and recliner. I crouch down, bringing myself more eye level than when I tower over her. "You're family, I step in and help anyone this way with no expectations of being repaid. Please don't think my offer comes with strings attached. I just want what's best for you, if I can help provide that, then so be it."

"You really are a good man; whatever woman convinces you to settle down is going to be one lucky lady," she tells me. "I'll go with you," she states matter of factly.

"Good," I tell her as I lean forward and press my lips to her forehead.

"I think you going out to California with Tristan is the best thing for you. Get you out of Boston and hopefully into a better environment," Jackson adds.

"I already talked to a couple of my teammates, and

their wives are waiting on the word you'll be coming back and are ready to welcome and befriend you."

"Just like that, no questions asked?" she asks.

"Avery, she's married to my team captain, Ryker, is one of the sweetest women you will ever meet. Will bend over backward to help you if she can. Then, there is her best friend who is married to another one of my teammates, Aiden. She's a bit more of a firecracker but is also really nice."

"They sound fun, and I can't wait to meet them," she says, a smile filling her face. Seeing her grin this way shoots straight to my heart, and I find myself wanting to find more ways to make it happen again.

CHAPTER 6
KENDRA

I STARE AT THE PILE OF BELONGINGS SITTING ON THE couch. Jackson and Tristan found someone who managed to get most of my things from Chad's place. I didn't ask questions because I didn't want to know exactly how they accomplished it or what happened while they were there. The less I think about him, the better. I keep having nightmares of that night, and the many other nights I slept with one eye open in fear for my life.

"Don't feel like you have to bring all of this with you if it brings back bad memories," Tristan says from where he leans against the wall. How he can tell what I'm thinking without me even saying a word is a bit freaky.

"I can't afford to replace any of it right now," I tell him honestly.

"Don't worry about it. I can take you shopping when we get there. It will be my starting over gift to you," he offers.

"I can't let you do that. You're already paying for my flight, giving me a place to live for free and food to eat. I'm never going to be able to pay you back for all of that, best yet, add on a shopping spree."

I watch as Tristan closes the distance between us. He crouches down, bringing his large body to be more in line with my height from sitting on the couch. His eyes are mesmerizing and can suck you into his trance in a matter of milliseconds. He gently wraps his hands around my left one. "I don't expect or want you to pay me back for helping you get back on your feet. You're family to me, Kendra. Let me help you."

I'm speechless, once again, at this man's kindness. Here, I always thought he was a badass playboy of a man, but really, he's just a big ass teddy bear. I'm sure the hockey groupies would love to know that tidbit of information.

I fidget with the hem of my T-shirt, not knowing how to respond to Tristan.

"Do you want anything that is laid out?" Tristan asks. The calmness of his voice soothes my racing heart, helping me not feel so agitated.

"I'm not sure yet, I haven't really looked through much of it. My heart started racing, and it was getting hard to breathe, so I was just staring off into space when you came in," I tell him honestly.

"Fair enough. I've got two options for you. One, I'll pack everything up and take it straight to the dumpster, never for you to worry about again. Or two, I pack it all into a suitcase and we take it with us. When you think you're ready to look at it, we pull it out and you can go through things then."

"What if I can't ever do it?" I whisper my question.

"Then we toss the suitcase, unopened, when you're ready," he says.

I chew on my bottom lip, not sure what the correct thing to do is. My mind is going about a thousand miles a minute. I just need to shut it off for a little while so that I can rest. "Okay, pack it up and we'll take it with us," I finally decide. This way, I can build up the nerve to look through all my things. Things that will remind me of him. Of the tough times that far outnumbered the good.

"Will do," Tristan says as he leans in and presses a kiss to my forehead. The contact of his lips against my skin sends a bolt of electricity down my entire body, causing me to shake slightly. "You okay?" he asks as he stands back up to his full height.

"Yeah, I'm fine," I manage to get out. "Just a slight chill ran through me."

"Are you still okay with leaving tomorrow?" Tristan asks. I know he was looking at ticket options earlier for us to fly to California.

"Besides Jackson and our parents, I don't have anything else tying me here, so I'm ready when you are."

"Sounds good. I should have our flight information within a few hours. The team's travel department is helping me find the best deals." He slips his phone out of his pocket, looking at the flashing screen. "That's them, I better take this," he says before stepping away as he puts his phone to his ear.

I relax against the back of the couch, my heart no longer feeling like it's going to thump right out of my chest now that my heart rate has returned to normal. I still don't know what I did to deserve Tristan's help, but I've come to terms with accepting it. I run my palm against my stomach, over the tiny baby that is inside there. I'm still wrapping my mind around the idea that I'm pregnant, which is going to make things interesting, really fast, living with Tristan. I know he's said that I can stay at his place for as long as I need to, but I have to wonder if he's thought about what it will be like once I have this baby. Is he going to want a random woman and her newborn hanging around when he's trying to bring women home? I can feel my pulse climbing again as I think about being out by myself with a newborn, and the panic starts to set in once again.

"Shit," I hear a voice say as the room goes fuzzy. "Kendra, I need you to take a few deep breaths, can you do that for me?"

I attempt to follow his lead, but it isn't doing much as my body attempts to breathe quickly, only dragging in small amounts of oxygen at a time, which in turn makes my pulse race even more.

I continue to try and match Tristan's breaths. He's keeping them steady and calm, and eventually, my body syncs with his.

"That's my girl," he says soothingly. I notice his hands touching my arms as they rub up and down, trying to comfort me as I recover from the panic attack. "Did something spook you?" he asks.

"Just my current life situation," I tell him vaguely, not wanting to admit my fears about him getting sick of me and my unborn child that lead to him kicking us out.

"Nothing to worry about, I've got everything covered," he assures me.

"I know, it just hit me out of nowhere."

"Good news, I got our flights for tomorrow," he says, changing the subject.

"That was fast."

"Doesn't usually take long to book flights, but the ones we got are pretty unique." He smiles at me, and I can tell he's up to something.

"What does that mean?" I ask.

"Because of all the travel that the team books, they have some connections with a private scheduler, and they found a trip where the plane is empty but needed back in California, so I booked it."

My jaw must about hit the floor. Did he just say private? I've dreamed of flying that way but never thought that my wish could come true. "Private, like, how small of a plane are we talking about?"

"Not sure of the specifics, other than it was cheaper to book this than one of the commercial flights we were looking at. Most people don't realize that you can book on people's private jets all the time."

"When do we leave?"

"Flight takes off at three tomorrow, they want us there at two thirty."

"I thought you had to be at the airport two hours before a flight?"

"For commercial, you do, but with private, you show up to a much smaller terminal. Some have a metal detector, but some don't since most people arriving are flying on their planes and can take whatever they want with them."

I shake my head in amazement. "I guess I never thought of that. It's not like I've ever had the opportunity to fly on a private plane before."

"We take chartered flights for all our away games, so I'm used to it," Tristan says, like it's just another daily thing for him, and I guess it kind of is. Another reminder of how different our lives are.

I LOOK AROUND MY BROTHER'S PLACE, MAKING SURE I haven't missed anything. Jackson and Tristan took care of packing up all the items they picked up for me that I just couldn't bear going through yet and have that suitcase set aside to come with us. I know I'll need to go through the things, but I just can't yet. When I looked at the items yesterday, it took me right back to that night. The yelling. The pain. The memories of just wanting to die so it would end.

I swipe at my face, catching the few tears that have managed to fall. I'm so over crying about Chad and how badly my life has spiraled because of him. I suck in a shaky breath, today is a new day. A fresh start for my life. I promise myself that I won't ever go back to that type of situation, and today is the first day of the rest of my life.

I hear the guys' voice in the other room and know that it is probably time to get going.

"Are you ready?" Tristan asks as I enter the living room.

"Yep, just making sure I didn't forget anything."

"Sounds good." He flashes me a smile that does things to my body. "You ready, bro?" he asks Jackson.

I look over at my brother and notice a small suitcase next to the couch where he's sitting. I'm confused by the sight of it as I'm not aware of him going anywhere.

"Where are you off to?" I ask him.

"With the two of you," he says, pointing to both Tristan and me. "Since he booked the private jet, he asked if I wanted to come out for a few days. I've got PTO at work, so I jumped at the offer. I've got a one-way ticket already booked for later in the week," he explains.

I love the fact my brother will be coming with us. I was dreading leaving him. He's been my rock these last few days, and I don't know how I'm going to survive with him on the other side of the country.

"It will be nice having you for a few more days," I tell him as I walk into his open arms for a hug I so desperately need. The safety I feel once inside his embrace is like a balm to my soul.

"Uber is about a minute out, so we need to head outside," Tristan says. Jackson releases his grip on me, and we all grab our bags, heading for the door.

The ride to the airport goes by in a blur. Tristan

wasn't lying when he said security at the private terminal was a breeze. They didn't care about liquids in our bags, or removing our shoes.

"Welcome aboard, I'm Stacey. Can I get any of you something to drink before we take off?" the flight attendant offers.

"I'll take a Sprite, if you have one," I tell her. My stomach has been a little testy today and I feel like I could vomit at any moment. I'm not sure if it's the nerves hitting me because of this major life change, the nerves because I'm flying, or pregnancy nausea. For all I know, it's a combination of all three."

"Of course, anything to eat?" she offers.

"Do you happen to have any crackers? My stomach is a little upset," I tell her.

"Absolutely, I'll be right back," she says before turning and heading back to the little galley in the back. She returns just a minute later with a Sprite and a few different cracker packs. "Give these a try. If they don't help, I've got a few other things that might."

"Thank you," I tell her as I open a small package of Ritz crackers.

"Can I get either of you something?" she asks the guys, who are sitting behind me.

I zone them out as they order drinks, and pop in my earbuds and hit play on the audiobook I've been listening to lately.

"Kendra." I hear my name being called as a hand rubs up and down my arm.

I open my eyes, forgetting for a second I'm on a plane on my way to California.

"Hi," I groggily say and pull my earbuds out of my ears. The pressure in them tells me that we're already preparing to land.

"Hi, sorry to wake you, but we're about to land," Stacey tells me.

"No problem, thank you. I didn't realize I was so exhausted," I tell her.

"It happens all the time. I used to get really sleepy as soon as I'd get in the air, but I'm used to it now. How's your stomach holding up?" she asks.

"Better now, thanks for the crackers earlier."

"Anytime." She smiles at me as she collects the trash.

I watch as she takes her seat up front, then look behind me at the guys who are busy talking to one another.

Tristan notices me looking and I can't miss the way his lips turn up in an easy smile. "Hey, you. Have a good nap?" he asks.

"I guess so," I tell him, stretching my neck.

"We were planning on stopping and grabbing some dinner after we land, does that sound okay to you?" he asks.

"Yeah, I'm pretty hungry, so that sounds like a great plan," I tell him.

"I figured tomorrow we can head out to the grocery store and pick up whatever you want to have around; I don't have much."

"Okay," I agree, knowing that he isn't going to have it any other way.

Before I realize it, we've touched down on what is

probably the smoothest flight I've ever been on. I'm kind of bummed I slept through it all, as I can't imagine I'd ever get the chance to fly on a private plane ever again.

CHAPTER 7
TRISTAN

I WIPE THE SWEAT FROM MY FACE, THEN TOSS THE SWEATY T-shirt to the side. Five miles on the treadmill at a little over five miles an hour has a tendency to get my blood pumping and my body going for a good workout, and heaven knows I need one after the last week.

"Fuck, man," Jackson curses from the machine beside me. "How the fuck do you do that?" He pants as he slows his machine down.

I chuckle at his discomfort and smirk. "Time and dedication, my man. Plus, all the time I spend on the ice. Helps build up that stamina."

"Yeah, sure, the time on the ice," he quips back. "You are sure it's not all that time you spend in bed with random women?"

"The stamina I've built from the ice definitely helps with the bed time." I flash him a shit-eating grin. He's a man and knows exactly what it's like. Neither one of us has found the woman who makes us want to settle down and do the relationship thing.

"On a serious note, can you cool it with the random women you bring home for a little while, with Kendra at your place?"

"Yeah, man, I can do that. Probably would be uncomfortable for all of us, so I'll keep this a safe place for her. You know I wouldn't do anything on purpose to hurt her, she'll be safe here. I promise you that," I sincerely tell my best friend. "I'd cut off my left nut before I'd let something happen to her here," I add for emphasis.

"No need to go cutting off your precious nuts, but thanks, man. I just need her safe," he tells me as we slap hands and pull one another into a sweaty man-hug.

Jackson and I have been best friends since we were in elementary school, so our ties run deep and are strong. I know he'd be there for me in a heartbeat if I needed something, just as I'd drop everything to be there for him or his family.

"Are you ready to lift some weights, now?" I ask as I move from the treadmills to the weight rack.

"Just don't kill me." He smirks as we both grab appropriate weights and I walk him through my normal routine when I work out at home. One of the things I liked about this building was the large gym they have for everyone to use. It was actually set up with good quality equipment, and many times I'm the only one in here working out.

We finish up and make sure we've put everything back where it belongs. Nothing irritates me more than when I come in here and people have left shit out and don't pick up after themselves. I snag my discarded sweaty shirt from where I tossed it earlier and we make our way back to my condo.

"We're back," I call out to Kendra as we enter.

"I'm just making some lunch," she calls back from the kitchen. "Are you guys hungry?"

"Starving, whatcha making?" Jackson asks her as we approach the kitchen island.

I find her standing barefoot in my kitchen, and feel my heart rate kick up as I take her in. Her bruises have started to fade, and her smile comes out more. If you take away the visual signs of her attack, she's beautiful.

"A Cobb salad and some BLTs," she says, turning our way. I don't miss the way her eyes run down my half-naked body. Is that lust I see in her eyes as she takes in my ripped abs?

I groan at the thought of eating what she's making. "Damn, I might just have to hire you as my chef," I suggest.

"You don't have to hire me, it's the least I can do since you're allowing me to stay here for free."

I just shrug my shoulders in reply. "How long until lunch will be ready?" I ask. I'd like to wash the sweat off before sitting down.

"Bacon should be done in a few minutes, then I just have to assemble the sandwiches," she replies.

"I'm going to go grab a quick shower, feel free to start without me." I head for my bedroom, and straight into the bathroom. I drop my shorts and step into the shower, turning it on as I do so. The cold water hits my body and I curse out a string of words at the shocking temperature. It doesn't take long for the hot water to come barreling out of the shower head and rinse the soap suds off my skin.

I dry off just as quickly as I soaped up, then find some clean boxers, a pair of athletic pants, and a team T-shirt. I head out to the kitchen, tugging my shirt over my head as I go. I find a platter filled with a few sandwiches, all assembled and cut in half like they came from a deli. My mouth waters as I look at them. I grab a couple, place them on the plate left out for me, add a large helping of the salad from the bowl to my plate, and take it to the table.

"Thank you for all this," I tell Kendra as I take the seat next to her.

"Figured sticking with something healthy would be your preference. Is there anything you don't like or want me to cook?" she asks as she takes a bite of salad.

"I'm not a fan of mushrooms or peas, but otherwise I'm not picky. But please don't feel obligated to cook for me."

"I don't mind, really. It also isn't like I have much else to do with my time. Once Jackson leaves, you'll be the only one I know here," she says quietly.

"You'll make friends in no time," I assure her.

"I need to figure out a job, insurance, and finding a doctor." She blows out a breath, one big enough the hairs around her face move with the air.

I pull out my cell, an idea hitting me that will hopefully tick a few of her needs off the list. I tap my text thread for Ryker and his wife, Avery, and send them both a message.

> Hey, you guys busy tonight?

AVERY

Just hanging out, what's up?

> I'm back in town with my friend's sister. I'd like to introduce her to a few of you, help her start to make some connections and maybe some girlfriends. She also needs some help with finding a good doctor and maybe a few other things. Is that something you could maybe help with?

RYKER

We could get together.

AVERY

Of course! What's her name?

> Kendra

AVERY

Give her my cell number and have her text me! I'll help any way I can.

> Thanks Avery, you're the best.

AVERY

I know {winky face}

"Are you up to meeting some of my friends tonight? They've offered to help you acclimate to the area. Assist you with whatever you need," I ask Kendra.

"Oh, yeah, I guess so," she says. I don't miss it when she runs her fingers over the bruise and swelling still surrounding her eye.

"Would you prefer to have them come here or do you want to get out?"

"Is here okay?" she asks quietly.

"Of course, whatever you're most comfortable with."

> Let's plan to get together at my place, maybe around 4:30 or so. We can throw some food on the grill or order in.

RYKER

> Works for us, Ellie might be home by then, is it okay if she tags along?

> Of course, I was going to text Aiden as well, see what they're up to.

AVERY

> No need, they're here and say they're in.

> {laughing emoji} okay then. See y'all later.

"Another one of my teammates and family are going to come over, as well. Ryker's teenage daughter, Ellie, might also tag along. You'll like her, she's pretty cool."

"You have teammates old enough to have teenage kids?" Kendra asks, scrunching her brows together as she considers her question.

"He's in his thirties, and he was early in his career when she was born, I believe. Her living with him only happened when he got picked up in the expansion draft. Before that, she always lived with her mom out here in California and he'd see her during the off-season or when he'd have road trips out here."

"Wow, that sounds like quite the adjustment."

"Her mom was transferred not long after he got here. They left it up to Ellie where she wanted to be, and since all her friends were here, she chose to stay with Ryker. He had to find someone who could help out with Ellie when he'd go on the road, and that's how he met his wife."

"Aww, that's sweet."

"She was his next-door neighbor. Stepped in at the last minute for a road trip when the arrangements they had set up fell through. I guess Ellie really took to Avery and then helped push them together, so it's been an easy transition for all of them."

"That's awesome. I can only imagine it isn't easy finding someone when you're a single parent," Kendra says, then drops her hand to her still-flat stomach. "Guess I'll find out just how hard that can be at some point in my life." Her voice sounds sad.

"The right man is out there for you, you just have to have faith," I tell her. I reach over and give her hand a quick squeeze.

"Damn this is good." Jackson breaks the silence that has fallen over us. He's still in the kitchen, obviously having taken a bite of something before he could make it to the table to join us.

"Only the best for my two favorite guys," Kendra calls out to him.

"A few of the guys and their significant others are coming over later to hang out, and have dinner," I tell him. "I want to introduce Kendra to them, help her start to make some girlfriends so she's not alone when I have to head out on road trips."

"Cool, anything I can do to help get ready?" Jackson asks.

"I might run down to the store and grab something to toss onto the grill."

"I can make some sides, if you like," Kendra offers.

"Maybe, let me see what I can find at the store, and we'll go from there."

"Okay," she gives in easily.

"HEY, MAN." I CLASP RYKER'S HAND AND PULL HIM INTO a man-hug before giving Avery and Ellie a hug as I welcome them into my place. "Thanks for coming over."

"Thanks for having us," Avery says as she holds up a dessert platter.

"Damn, you're going to really make sure I have to hit the gym every day this week."

"I'm sure you can handle a cookie or two." She smirks.

"Let me introduce you," I tell them as we walk further into my place. Kendra and Jackson are both in the living room. I take in Kendra, first, and can tell that she's nervous. Her hands are folded together but I can see her fingertips as they rub circles on the tops of her hands. "Ryker, Avery, and Ellie, I'd like you to meet my best friend, Jackson Torres, and his sister, Kendra Torres."

"Nice to meet you," Ryker says to Jackson as they shake hands. Avery makes her way over to Kendra and drops down on the couch next to her.

"It's so nice to meet you," Avery says in her calming way. Ellie follows suit, sitting next to Avery.

"Hi, I'm Ellie." She offers a little wave.

"Hi, nice to meet you," Kendra tells both women. "Thanks for coming over today. Tristan picked up some stuff for the grill, so I hope everyone is hungry."

"Oh, honey, these guys can eat," Avery laughs. "There's a reason they have to pay them so well. They need it to cover the grocery bills."

Kendra's eyes widen slightly before she laughs along with Avery. That laugh has her relaxing into the couch and I release the breath I was holding. Maybe, just maybe, my idea of bringing her out here wasn't such a bad idea, after all.

We all fall into a comfortable conversation, the girls all getting to know one another better and the guys talk about the upcoming season. Aiden and Tori, along with their son, Carter, arrive, and after another round of introductions, we fall right back into socializing.

CHAPTER 8
KENDRA

I WATCH WITH CLOSE ATTENTION AS TORI SITS AND bounces Carter in her lap. He's such a cute baby and it makes me think about my own baby. The one currently the size of a bean, if the internet is to be believed.

"Would you like to hold him," she asks.

"Oh, sure," I say, holding out my hands. None of my friends or Chad's had kids, so my experience around them is pretty slim. I nervously take Carter into my hands and let him bounce his little legs on the top of my thighs like his mom was doing. He giggles as he tries to shove his entire fist into his mouth, his drool dribbling out of his mouth and onto my shirt.

"He's teething like no other, sorry about that," Tori says as she reaches over and wipes his face with the bib that is hanging off his neck.

"It's okay." I giggle at him. He's such a cute little one. "Is he usually this happy about teething?" I ask.

"Only during the day. At night, it's usually crying until the numbing gel and Tylenol kick in," Tori says.

"I keep telling her a little whiskey to the gums will knock him right out," Aiden adds, "but I just get the evil eye when I make those kinds of suggestions." He laughs.

"I'm not going to give our baby alcohol." She rolls her eyes. "Even if our grandmothers swear by it," she says to Aiden before turning back my way. "As soon as you have kids, everyone wants to give you their two cents on how best to raise them. It can be a little nauseating, at times, but they usually mean well."

"I don't know anything about babies, but I need to learn pretty fast," I find myself telling Tori.

"Oh, are you expecting?" she asks as her eyes widen and a smile fills her face.

"Yeah, that was probably the biggest surprise when I was in the hospital. When they ran my bloodwork, I guess it's standard they check so they know for sure. I didn't know until the doctor came in to talk to me about my injuries."

"Can you recommend a doctor we can get her in with?" Tristan asks, inserting him into our conversation.

"Of course, I love my doctor," Tori tells both of us. "Even if this little man couldn't wait to make his appearance for her to deliver him," she chuckles.

"Oh, who delivered him, then?" I ask.

"I did," Aiden pipes up. "Well, and his momma." He comes to stand by her side, leaning down, he places a kiss on her cheek. "He was born at home, in the tub."

"Wow, that must have been scary."

"Not so scary as it was painful," Tori tells me. "I'd been having Braxton hicks contractions for weeks, which I was assured were normal. That day, they were constant and then quickly turned into much stronger contractions. By the time I yelled for Aiden, it was too late and, minutes later, Carter made his appearance. The paramedics arrived shortly after and got us to the hospital so we could be checked out. Thankfully, nothing went wrong, and we were released in the normal amount of time spent in the hospital after delivery."

"Sounds like something you won't ever forget."

"That's for sure. Hopefully, when we have the next one, I'll have a little more notice and I can do it with drugs."

"You were a rockstar," Aiden tells her.

"Do you know when your due date is?" Avery asks.

"I don't remember if they gave me a due date. They said the ultrasound put me at about seven weeks, but that was about a week ago."

"What's your cell number? I'll text you my doctor's contact info and you can call their office first thing tomorrow and let them know I referred you. Hopefully, they can get you in ASAP."

I rattle off my number to Tori as she adds it to her phone, seconds later, my phone pings with a contact for the doctor. I also get another text from Avery just saying hi and that I can call or text her anytime I need something. Tears threaten to form at the kindness of these two women who I've known for a whopping hour so far.

"Thank you, I'll call them first thing," I tell her as I save the contact as well as add both of their numbers as saved ones in my phone. I went through all my contacts yesterday, removing ones I no longer need now that I'm finally away from Chad. I hope to never have to see him again, nor any of his friends. Just thinking of them makes my stomach roll. The shit I put up with for so long might take me a while to come to terms with, but I know I'm safe here and won't ever be subject to that kind of treatment ever again.

I can't get over how relaxed I am around this group of people. The longer we all hang out, the more I feel like we've been friends forever. The guys all retreated outside when it was time to fire up the grill. Tristan picked up some kabobs at the store. Apparently, they had cooked up some and they were sampling them to customers. Perfect way to advertise the sale they had going as he bought a big package of them. He also picked up some pre-made sides from the deli counter, not wanting to make me feel obligated to cook for everyone.

"Damn, these are good," Tori says as she eats her way through one of the kabobs. "We might need to stop at the store on the way home and pick more up," she tells Aiden.

"Whatever you want, dear." He smiles at his wife. Seeing the kind of love that they have for one another makes me long for that kind of connection with some-one. I see the same thing when I look at Avery and Ryker. My eyes drift over to Tristan and find him watching me intently. I swear I see them darken when our eyes connect. I can feel myself being pulled toward him but slam any thoughts of that from my mind. He doesn't think of me like that. I'm his best friend's little sister and now a soon-to-be single mom. He'd never think of me any other way.

"All right, we should get little man home and into bed," Aiden says as he picks up a sleepy Carter from where he's sitting on the floor, playing with some toys.

"We should head out, as well," Avery says. "I've got an early work call in the morning."

"Text me and let me know what Dr. Morgan's office says. Even if she can't get you in, all the doctors there are amazing."

"I'll let you know for sure. Thanks for their contact info."

"Of course. And if you need a ride to the appointment or anywhere, just let one of us know."

"That's so kind of you to offer. I was just planning on figuring out the bus schedule, I don't want to be a burden on anyone."

"No way, definitely not a burden."

"I can swing by and pick up Tristan if he wants to just leave you with his car," Ryker offers.

"That's a great idea. I'm not sure why I didn't think of it already," Tristan says before I can decline the offer.

"Oh, that works even better," Tori says as I sit here just opening and shutting my mouth with no words or sound coming out. Once again, tears burn the back of my eyes, thanks to their kindness.

"It was great to meet you, welcome to the clan," Ryker says, giving me a side hug as everyone says their goodbyes.

"Thank you, it was great to meet everyone. Ellie is

so awesome, I'm sure you're proud of her," I tell him and he preens at the compliment about his daughter.

"She's the best, I definitely won in the parent lottery."

Once everyone is gone, the guys retreat to the living room, while I head to the kitchen. I start rinsing the plates and adding them to the dishwasher. "Stop," Tristan says sternly from the doorway. My body stiffens at his tone, and he must notice the way I flinch. "Fuck," he mumbles. "I didn't mean it in a bad way, sorry if that came out wrong. I just don't want you feeling like you have to clean up after my friends. I can get it in just a bit, come relax in the living room. Spend some time with your brother before he has to go home tomorrow."

I place the plate that is still in my hands into the dishwasher, then close it up and step away from the sink. I know deep down his hard tone wasn't directed at me in anger, but that was my body's first reaction and I hate that it was.

Tristan stops me before I can walk past, his hand raised in the air as he contemplates if he should touch me or not. He ends up resting it on my arm, the touch soft, but the electrical current his touch sends through my body wakes me up in ways I haven't ever experienced. "I'm sorry," I whisper, hoping like hell I don't start crying in front of him. "I know you'd never hurt me, but I can't help my automatic response to certain things."

"You have nothing to apologize for, I'll do better going forward."

We stand there, just staring at one another for a few

seconds before Tristan drops his hand from my arm. I quickly walk out and into the living room, taking a seat on the couch next to my brother. He wraps an arm around my shoulders and pulls me into a sitting side hug. "You going to be okay staying here? I can buy you a ticket and you can come back with me tomorrow, if needed."

"I'll be fine. I think the new start will be good for me," I tell him honestly. "And you know I'm safe with Tristan around."

"No one else I'd trust more with your safety," Jackson says as he kisses the top of my head. I really hit the sibling jackpot with Jackson. We might have fought like cats and dogs when growing up, but the older we got, the closer we got. I almost ruined that when I started dating Chad, but, thankfully, Jackson looked past my mistakes and was at my side the moment I needed him most.

CHAPTER 9
TRISTAN

THE PAST WEEK HAS FLOWN BY. I'M NOT REQUIRED TO return for another week, but those of us that are back in town have been meeting up at the practice rink most days to work out and to get some drills in, so we're ready when training camp does start, and the coaches run us until we're puking. With Jackson back in Boston, it's just been Kendra and me at the condo the past few days. It's definitely an adjustment, having someone else there all the time. Someone to hang out with, watch shows with, and have meals with. Meals she insists on cooking for the two of us. The only thing I don't have is someone sharing my bed and that's been an adjustment to get used to. I'm ashamed to admit just how many times I've rubbed one out in the shower thinking about her. Thoughts that I need to push from my mind. I'm here to help her move on, find a way to make a new life and eventually move out on her own when she's stable and ready to do so.

"You headed straight home, or do you want to stop and grab some lunch?" Ryker asks as we both get dressed in the locker room.

"I'm easy, what are you thinking?" I ask.

"Avery is at a meeting, so no need to rush home," he says, and now I understand his no-rush attitude today. He normally wants to get home as quickly as possible. Claims he has to take advantage of the hours when they're kid-free, thanks to the school day. I've never had to take into consideration what time it is or who's around when I have sex, so I just take his word for it.

"Let's grab some lunch. Kendra has my car today and an appointment with the doctor Tori recommended."

"How's that going?" he asks.

"Fine, why wouldn't it?" I ask.

"Nothing between the two of you?" he asks and quirks a brow.

"No," I say sternly and shut that line of questioning down as quickly as I can. "She's Jackson's little sister, I'd never cross that line," I add for emphasis.

"You're both consenting adults, nothing wrong with it if you were to have more," he says.

"Not happening. She needs time to heal. I don't know all the details, and I don't need to because what I do know just pisses me off and the dude is lucky the cops found him first, or else I might be sitting behind bars for the rest of my life. But the last thing she needs right now is a relationship."

"If you say so. My wife thinks the two of you both

have feelings for each other that are deeper than just friends."

"I think she's looking at things through rose-colored glasses. Still has that newlywed love clouding her judgment."

"Nothing wrong with that," he smiles. "That cloud gets me laid most days."

"I need to get laid," I groan. "That is definitely something that I need to do sometime soon."

He just laughs at my expense as he continues to get dressed.

We hit up a pub not far from the practice facility. They've got good food and are great about letting us sit in their banquet room if it's not in use. If it is, they try and give us a back booth for a little privacy while we eat. While I don't mind talking to fans and signing autographs, it's also nice to eat in peace and not be bombarded with people coming up to us interrupting every few minutes.

"Damn, that hit the spot," Ryker says as we head back out to his car.

"Sure did," I tell him as I check my phone. Nothing from Kendra, which I'm not sure if that's a good or bad sign. I know she had a doctor's appointment this morning, so I was kind of hoping she'd let me know how that went, but maybe she's just waiting until I get home to tell me about it.

"Same time tomorrow?" Ryker asks as he pulls into the parking lot of my condo.

"Works for me." I bump his outstretched fist before

climbing out of his truck and making my way inside. I slide my key into the lock, turning it easily before opening the door. The smell of something sweet hits my nose and instantly has my mouth watering.

"What smells like heaven?" I ask as I walk in, coming to a stop at the kitchen island. I watch Kendra as she pulls a pan from the oven, some kind of cookie filling the pan.

"Cookies!" She smiles up at me, and my heart fucking flutters in my chest. "I had a craving for some, so stopped at the store after my appointment to grab what I needed and didn't think you'd have. As soon as I got back, I got to work and made a big batch."

"They smell amazing, can I have one?" I ask, reaching for a steaming hot cookie. She smacks at my hand before I can touch one.

"Not one of those, you'll burn yourself," she says as she hands me a cookie from a rack on the counter I didn't even notice until she reached for it. "Basic chocolate chip," she says as I take my first bite, moaning as I do. "I've got oatmeal chocolate chip going in next. I couldn't decide between the two, so I made some of each."

"You're going to be the death of my healthy meal plan, but these cookies are worth it," I tell her around my last bite of the warm and gooey cookie.

"If it's a problem to have sweets in the house, I can hold back on baking," she says nervously.

"No, it's not a problem, I promise. I'm just a weak man when it comes to baked goods. An extra mile on the treadmill to burn off the calories will be well worth the indulgence." I wink at her as I reach for a second cookie.

"How was practice?" she asks as she moves the hot cookies off the sheet and onto the rack with the others.

"Good. Camp hasn't started yet, so not everyone is back. But it's felt good to get back out on the ice, get the blood pumping through my legs on a daily basis. It will make the first few days of camp not as bad."

"Are you guaranteed to make the team?" she asks.

"Yeah." I smile at her question. "My last contract came with the perks of adding in trade limits. I've been playing long enough that I can't be sent back down to the AHL without clearing waivers, and not to sound conceited, but that just won't happen anytime soon."

"What does clearing waivers mean?"

"Once a guy has played a certain number of NHL games, in order to be eligible to be sent down a level, he must first be put on waivers. It lasts twenty-four hours. If, at any point, in that twenty-four hours, another team wants to pick him up, they can do so, and it doesn't cost them anything except his salary. So unlike a trade with another team, the team he plays for gets nothing except him off their roster. It is a gamble for teams to put someone on waivers, but sometimes it is their only option if someone is coming off the injured reserve list or long-term list, and because of that, they'll be over the cap limit. It can all be a bit confusing, but it happens occasionally. Most of the time, the guys that are being called up only do so for a few games, then get sent back down, so they don't have to clear waivers because they don't hit the threshold. Some teams will game the system by sending a guy down to the AHL on paper as soon as a game ends, but he doesn't actually report to that team. Then, hours before the next game, they file the paperwork to call him back up. They do this because every day he isn't on the active roster is one day less that his NHL salary is making an impact on the team's cap space and stops and restarts that clock for having to clear waivers."

"That sounds so confusing."

"I'm sure it does to someone who isn't used to it being part of their job, but that's enough about hockey. How was your appointment?" I ask.

"It was good, I saw the doctor Tori recommended, and she was so nice. She was able to get my records from the hospital to have in my chart. She did a quick ultrasound and I'm due mid-April."

"Do you know yet if it's a girl or boy? Do you even want to find out?"

"Still way too early, probably another ten or eleven weeks before I can find out. I can't see why I wouldn't, but I've got time to decide. She gave me the information I needed to try and get on Medicaid. They have a special division for pregnant women. I want to pull up their application and see what I can take care of online. They agreed to see me today without paying anything yet, but if I'm denied the maternity coverage, then I'll have to figure out a way to pay them."

"I can cover the costs for you," I tell her.

"I know you can, I just hate asking you. You've

already done so much for me. I don't want you to feel like I'm a burden."

"It's not a problem. I understand if you want to apply, but don't stress if they deny you. I wonder if there's a way I can add you to my insurance. It's got great coverage with low out-of-pocket expenses."

"I couldn't ever ask you to do that."

"You aren't asking me; I'm offering to look into it. For all I know, it isn't possible unless we were married, but if I ask, we'll at least know for sure."

"Let me see what this application entails, first, then, if I'm denied, we can look into the latter."

"I can live with that." I nod, emphasizing my words. "Do you need help with anything or am I good to go grab a shower?"

"I'm good." Kendra flashes me a smile. I've noticed she's done that more in the time she's been here. As the days go by, she seems to relax a little more, making my condo a home and not just a place she's visiting.

"Holler if you need anything, but I shouldn't be long." I tap my fist on the countertop twice before stepping away and heading for my room. The door clicks shut behind me, putting some space between the two of us. I'm not sure what it was about seeing her in my kitchen, baking, looking sexy with flour smudged on her cheek and that smile on her face. It did something to me.

I don't really need another shower since I took one at the rink after we worked out, but it was the only thing I could think of that was a reasonable reason I needed to get myself out of there and some distance between us. I walk straight for the shower and flip the water on, leaving it on the cold side. Maybe some cold water will snap me out of this trance I've suddenly found myself in.

I quickly strip out of my clothes, check that I've got a towel hanging up, and step under the cold spray. My body immediately revolts at the water temperature, goose bumps popping out all over the place as it reacts to the shock. I can't take more than a few seconds of the cold, so I reach ahead and turn the handle until the water is nice and hot. It thaws my cold skin, warming it all the way up.

I squirt some body wash out on my hand, rubbing it over my chest and arms. As my hand snakes down my torso, I can't ignore my straining cock. My palm shuttles over my length as I squeeze it tightly in my grip while I lean the other arm against the shower wall and put my weight into it as I stroke myself faster and faster. I try my damnedest to think about the night before I left for Boston when I had those two women here in my bed, but I'm having a hard time keeping those images playing. Instead, my mind wanders to Kendra. What she'd feel like wrapped around my cock. What kind of noises would she make if I took her up against this shower wall, or over the edge of my bed? Would she squirt all over my face if I licked her long enough?

"Fuck," I yell out, my orgasm barreling out of me as I cover the shower wall in cum.

I lean into the wall, my legs a bit shaky after coming so hard. I see stars behind my eyelids, so I take a moment to recover, then chastise myself as I clean the shower up and finish rinsing off for using thoughts of Kendra to get myself off. What in the hell was I thinking? She isn't here to be my fuck buddy, she's here because she needed help and a new start and that's something that I can give her.

CHAPTER 10
KENDRA

I LEFT MY APPOINTMENT WITH DR. MORGAN FEELING good. Finding out I was pregnant the way I did has made this experience strange, not that I know what finding out you're pregnant any other way feels like, as this is the first time. But I haven't felt that connected to it as it still feels so surreal. Dr. Morgan was so kind and took her time to really talk to me, asked a lot of questions, plus answered every single one of mine. All with no judgment at all. Even the tough ones, like abortion and adoption. While I considered the first option when I was still in the hospital, I decided it wasn't something I wanted to pursue. I'm also not sure about adoption. I'm twenty-four years old, not a teenager. Can I give a baby a good life? I'd like to think so. It might not be fancy, but I'd like to think that I'd be a good mom to this little one.

I felt weird taking money from Tristan, but he insisted that I have some on me in case I needed to buy something. Knowing that I had money in my wallet, when the craving for cookies hit as I was leaving the hospital, I decided a stop at the grocery store was in order.

I walked into that store with a pep in my step and grabbed the few things I needed that I was confident Tristan didn't have in his kitchen before I headed back and started baking. There was just something so soothing about creaming together all the ingredients, watching as they go from basic and bland to perfectly blended into a delicious concoction. As I stand in the kitchen, scooping cookies out onto the cookie sheets, I can see myself doing just this, but with a little girl standing on a stool beside me, helping me add things to the bowl as we make a huge mess.

When Tristan got home a little bit ago, I couldn't help but smile at the way he reacted to the cookie I let him eat. I could get lost in that man's eyes, and don't get me started on the little moans he lets out. They make me think of *other* moans and what that must sound like.

I shove those ideas out of my mind, moving instead to mixing the chocolate chips into the second bowl of batter, this being the oatmeal chocolate chip ones. I can faintly hear the water running in Tristan's bathroom but try to ignore it. If I focus on that, my mind will want to wander to the fact that he's *naked* in there, and that will only lead to trouble.

My timer goes off, alerting me to pull the pan from the oven. Just as I set it on the counter, I hear Tristan yell what sounds like "fuck" from the shower. I'm unsure what to do. Is something wrong? Has he hurt himself? I hesitate, not sure if I should say screw it and go in and check on him. I'd never forgive myself if he needed help and I just stayed out here doing nothing. I abandon the cookies for a minute and head over to his bedroom door. I press my ear against the wood, trying to hear anything else, but all I can hear is the sound of water. I take that as a good sign and chalk it up to him just dropping something, and go back to the kitchen to scoop out the next pan of cookies.

I'M LYING ON THE COUCH, WATCHING AN EPISODE OF *American Greed*, my mind blown at how shady people can be. Tristan is stretched out on the other side of the large piece of furniture. He's just as engrossed in the episode as I am.

"That's fucked up," he comments when the episode goes to commercial. "I don't know how people can live such double lives."

"Right, and how do they come up with these ideas to steal from people? Truly evil to do what they've done."

"It makes me not want to trust anyone, ever."

"Do you have people that help manage your money?" I ask, more curious about what it must be like to make so much money each year. I've never really made what would be considered a livable salary, mostly working entry-level jobs that pay the basic bills.

"Yeah, I was stupid in my first season or two, but then buckled down and got smart with my money. I know this job won't last me forever and I want to be set after it ends. That's not to say I won't find something to do once I can no longer play, but I don't want to be feeling like I have to find something right away just to keep a roof over my head and food in the fridge."

"That's smart. How long do you think you'll play?" I ask.

He chuckles. "Isn't that the magic fucking question every professional athlete would like to know going into their career." He sits up a little, rubbing the back of his neck as he turns his attention my way. "I'll play as long as I possibly can. Thankfully, I'm pretty healthy. I haven't had any major injuries, a few pulled muscles that had me out a handful of games."

"Am I remembering correctly that you had to have surgery a few years ago?"

"Ah, yes, my appendix ruptured about two years ago now. Emergency surgery fixed me all up," he says as he lifts his T-shirt up to show me the scar on his abdomen. "Thankfully, that happened just after the season ended. I was all healed up by the time camp came back around a few months later."

"That's good, any other surgeries?"

"My tonsils when I was a kid, but otherwise, I'm as healthy as they come. What about you?" he asks.

"Just my wisdom teeth when I was in high school."

Tristan laughs, his eyes dancing with humor as he looks at me. "I almost forgot about that, you were so high on the pain meds."

"Ugh, don't remind me. I really hope Jackson

deleted the videos he took of me making an ass out of myself."

"I'm going to ask him." Tristan laughs and grabs his phone.

"Don't you dare!" I try and nudge him with my foot, but it does no good. He just smiles as he taps out a text message on his phone to my brother.

"Too late," he grins. "Just think of how fun it will be to watch it again."

"Fun for you, maybe," I huff, trying to hold back my laughter. It only works for a few seconds before I'm cracking a smile and laughing right along with him. This feels so good. I can't tell you the last time I was this carefree or felt this relaxed and safe.

"Hell yes!" Tristan bellows as he sits up and shakes his phone. "He sent me the video, come here and let's reminisce at your expense."

"I sure hope he has some embarrassing videos of you saved somewhere," I retort as I sit up and move to be next to him. Once I'm settled, he turns his phone sideways, so the video fills the screen, and hits play. We both watch, laughing as I jabber on about random things that make no sense while still affected by the anesthesia they gave me for my surgery.

"That wasn't so bad, was it?" he asks once we've finished watching it for a second time.

"I guess it wasn't that bad," I admit.

We continue to reminisce about our childhoods and how much life has changed. Tristan missed some of our growing up years as he was playing hockey in different places. I remember how hard that first season was for

Jackson when he was gone in another state, living with a strange family as he pursued his dream of playing professional hockey.

He tells me stories of his billeting days. How it was an adjustment to living in someone else's house, but how he still to this day stays in contact with those families, and how they still follow his career. Coming out to support him when he plays near them, or even taking vacations to see him play. Kind of crazy how tight-knit the hockey community is, when you think of it.

"I meant to ask you earlier, was everything okay in the shower? I could have sworn I heard you yell out fuck, but then didn't hear anything else. I wasn't sure if you needed help or what?" I ask him.

His body goes stiff for a split second. If I wasn't right next to him, I probably wouldn't have noticed it, but since I am, I did.

"You heard that?" he asks, his voice low and gravely.

"Yes?" I say, but it sounds like a question. "Was I not supposed to?" My eyebrows pull together. Now, I'm really confused as to why me hearing him call out from the shower would be a problem.

"Just surprised to know the walls are that thin. But everything was fine, just dropped something on my foot," he says, but for some reason, I don't quite believe him.

"Is your foot okay?" I ask, looking down at the bare extremity.

"It's fine, just one of those things that hurts like a motherfucker for a few minutes and then is fine."

"If you say so." I give him a side-eye.

"I think I'm going to call it a night," Tristan says as he stands up and stretches.

I glance at the clock and see that it is only eight. "This early?" I cock a brow at him.

He looks at the clock, realizing that it is still early. "Shit, I thought it was much later than it is," he admits and plops back down on the couch. "Want to turn on a movie or something?"

"I'm easy," I tell him, and regret it as soon as it leaves my lips. The way his eyes flare tells me he took it just as it sounded. He just grunts and makes himself comfortable again. I move back to the other side of the couch, getting as comfortable as I possibly can. I'm not sure what is happening between the two of us, but something is. I just hope that it doesn't burn me like so many other things in my life have.

CHAPTER 11
TRISTAN

I TRY AND GET COMFORTABLE ON THE COUCH. IT ISN'T EASY with Kendra on the other side, looking all cozy in her yoga pants and tank top. I can't believe she heard me in the shower. It makes me wonder what else she can hear when I'm locked in my bedroom.

We settle on an old comedy, but I don't pay it any attention as I lay here thinking about what the hell I'm doing, lusting after Kendra. She's got enough shit on her plate, she doesn't need me adding more to it.

The movie ends, finally at a reasonable hour to head to bed. I need good sleep tonight for all the time I'm going to spend in the gym tomorrow. I guess one way to get her out of my system is to sweat it out. Either that or I need to call a fuck buddy and see if they'll meet me at their place or a hotel or some shit like that. Maybe getting laid is what I need. Release some endorphins and get myself back to normal.

"Have a good night," Kendra calls from the couch as I make my way toward my room.

I'm such a dick. I didn't even say anything to her as I got up. "Night," I call over my shoulder. It was still a dick thing to do, but I need the space.

I WRAP MY HANDS BEFORE SLIDING THEM INTO THE BOXING gloves that are kept in a bin near the bag. Not all the guys like to use the punching bag, but I need it today.

"Damn, man, what's got you all worked up?" Aiden asks as he steps up beside the bag.

"Nothin'," I huff out between heavy breaths.

"Why don't I believe you?" He chuckles.

I just grunt as I punch the bag faster, feeling the burn in my muscles as I give it everything I have in me until failure. I drop to the mat, sucking in large lungsful of air as I attempt to catch my breath and lower my heart rate.

"Want to rethink that answer?" he asks as he offers me the bottle of water I'd left off to the side.

"Not really. Just trying to work it out of my system without fucking shit up," I tell him after I've caught my breath.

"If you want to talk about it, you know where to find me," he offers before wandering away. I know my friends mean well, but fuck, can't a guy just wallow in his own shit for a while as he figures out what he's going to do?

I take the boxing gloves off, tossing them back into the bin. I've run my body hard today. An hour on the ice running drills, five miles on the treadmill, followed by another hour of weights, and now the bag. My muscles are screaming at me that I'm done.

I head for the locker room, stripping down to my boxers so I can take a dip in the ice bath. The shock to my system is exactly what I need after the torture I put my body through today. I sit for as long as I can handle the cold, then head for the showers so I can get out of here for the day.

I walk into my condo, but instead of being greeted by the smell of freshly baked cookies, today, I'm met by a dark and quiet space. I realize just how much I enjoyed yesterday's arrival and was looking forward to a similar one today.

"Kendra," I call out as I walk further into my place.

I don't hear anything, and panic starts to set in. Where is she? Is everything okay? I didn't leave her my car today as she said she didn't need to go anywhere. I head for her bedroom and that's exactly where I find her, fast asleep on her bed, iPad next to her like she fell asleep while on it. I stand at her doorway like a creeper, watching as she sleeps so peacefully. Her hair is fanned out on the pillow, her skin looking so creamy. What would it be like to be able to crawl in next to her, pull her into my arms, and fall asleep just like that.

I watch for a few seconds longer, leaving her to sleep. Now that I know she's safe, I don't need to be a creep for any longer than I already have been.

I keep myself busy by flipping through a local Taylor's website looking at suits. I need a few new ones for the upcoming season. I like to replace a few every season; helps keep things fresh with how often I have to wear them during the season. One thing I've learned to splurge on since securing a spot on an NHL roster is nice suits. The cheap ones start showing their wear and tear after just a few months, and with a season that lasts as long as ours does, especially if we make it deep into the playoffs, I need ones that will last.

I flag a few and send them off to the store's email so they can have them ready for my appointment next week. They already have my measurements, so they usually will have ones my size if in stock, ready for me to try on when I come in, and it makes the appointment go that much faster for all of us.

"Hey," Kendra says, pulling my attention from my iPad. I didn't even hear her get up. "When did you get back?" She takes a seat on the recliner.

"An hour or so ago?" I say, checking the time.

"I must have fallen asleep researching the maternity insurance and trying to find a job." She covers a yawn as she relaxes back into the recliner.

"What did you find out?" I ask, realizing I never stopped at the team's office to ask about adding her to my insurance.

"Eligibility is based on household income. The baby is considered in the household numbers, but what I'm unsure of is how they'd take into consideration that you're letting me stay here, so I'm going to have to make an appointment and figure out if that makes me ineligible. It did say that if you rent, a copy of your lease is needed, so maybe we could say I rent a room?"

"Maybe," I say, and it comes out a little gruffer than

I expected. "What's this about looking for a job?" I ask after clearing my throat.

"I kind of need a way to make money, Tristan. I can't just mooch off of you for the rest of my life. I know I haven't had this baby yet, but from what I've researched, they aren't cheap. Like, at all. How do you expect me to be able to provide what this baby needs if I don't have money to pay for it?" She gives me a WTF face and I realize she's right.

"I know, I just don't want you stressing about finding something, especially something that will be easy on you as you progress further into your pregnancy. Isn't that hard on a woman's body?"

"It can be, but we were also made to handle growing a tiny human. Can't be any worse than what I've already lived through."

"Don't say that. What you lived through and survived can't be compared to anything else," I admittedly say.

"I sent in applications to a few temp agencies I found that had some secretary positions listed. I figured those couldn't be that hard," she says, ignoring my comment.

"Is that what you really want to do?" I ask.

"Not really, but it isn't like I can be picky right now."

"What is your dream job?" I ask, realizing I have no idea what her answer is going to be.

"A chef, but not in a demanding kitchen. I love making home-cooked meals with real ingredients, not reheating something that is half-processed crap."

"Like all the meals you've made for me?" I ask.

"Exactly." She smiles big as she answers.

"What if you made a business making small-batch meals for families? With how popular the mail meal companies are, I'm sure a local one would be just as successful. You can use my kitchen to cook and distribute."

"How would I even find clients?" she asks.

"Talk to Tori and Avery. I'm sure they could pass the word amongst the other wives. Many of them have kids, so if the meals are family-friendly, I'm sure some of the moms would love having heathy meals they only have to heat up on busy nights."

"It's an idea. But also sounds expensive to get going," she states.

"I could give you a loan, we'd write it up, make it official, if that makes you feel better," I suggest. "But like I said, you could use the kitchen here to get a start."

"Maybe," she says and that's at least a start. She isn't completely disregarding the idea.

"I'll be your first customer," I say to try and encourage the idea.

"No way am I charging you to cook for you. Hell, you're already paying for the food. Plus, me cooking was how we agreed I'd contribute to you letting me stay here."

"You do have a point. Okay, so I can't be your first customer, but I can be your taste tester."

She laughs and it's the most beautiful sound. "I'm always in need of one of those," she says. "Speaking of a taste tester, I'm trying out a new recipe for dinner tonight. An apple cider braised pork shoulder I found online. The pictures made it look so good."

"My stomach is already growling at the sound of that. Do we need anything at the store for it?" I ask.

"Nope, I added everything to the list the other day."

"Perfect. I still think you should look into the meal prep thing," I tell her once more, this time going a step further and tapping out a text message to my friends' wives.

> I had an idea for Kendra and want your opinions and possibly encouragement for her to try my idea out.

AVERY

> Are you going to keep us waiting?

TORI

> Spill the beans

> Hold your damn horses, I can only type so fast. LOL

> I asked her what her dream job was, and she said being a chef, but more a private one. My idea was for her to start a meal service. Provide busy families with a few home-cooked meals a week they can just heat up and know they have fresh ingredients and not something processed and filled with crap.

AVERY

> I love it! Where do I sign up?

TORI

Absolutely. I think the WAGs would fill
her books up, especially during the
season.

I thought the same damn thing, so
good to know we're on the same page.
Can you ladies work your magic and
convince her of the same thing. I've
already told her she's got free use of
my kitchen and I'll happily be her taste
tester for menus if she needs them.

AVERY

I'm sure you did. {smirking face}

TORI

On it.

You're both the best. Thanks for your
help with this.

I toss my phone on the coffee table, knowing that
my friends will work their magic and work on
convincing Kendra that she should entertain this idea.

"Speaking of dinner, I've got to get to work in the
kitchen as it takes a few hours to cook," she says as she
gets up. "Shit, I didn't realize it was already so late. I
needed it in the oven, like, two hours ago." She looks
between me and the kitchen, worrying her bottom lip
with her teeth.

"Then make it tomorrow. We can order some
takeout tonight."

"Are you sure?" she asks.

"Of course I'm sure. I'm not that big of an asshole
that you can't have a night off from making me dinner."

"Okay, I just feel bad since I had a plan, but that didn't include taking a nap mid-day."

"Better to listen to your body and rest when it needs it," I tell her.

"Yeah, I didn't sleep all that well last night. I tossed and turned most of the night trying to get comfortable."

"Is the bed okay? Do you need anything to make things better?" I ask, worried that she doesn't have what she needs.

"I'm fine, just an off night. I finally got up and took some melatonin and passed out. I think it was just my mind wouldn't shut off and let me fall asleep. Lots going on in here." She taps the side of her head with a finger.

"I understand that. What sounds good for dinner tonight?"

"Hmmm, I'm not sure. What are you thinking?"

"I'm open to anything. Not much I won't eat. There's a good Thai place a few blocks away that delivers, or a little Italian place. They have the best calzones I've ever had."

"That sounds good. A super cheesy calzone sounds perfect."

"Do you want anything else in it?"

"Do they have a barbecue chicken option?"

"I think so, let me pull up the menu. If not, I know you can build your own," I tell her as I pull up the website. "Looks like you're in luck, BBQ chicken comes with their homemade sauce, chopped chicken, onions, two types of cheese, and the top is drizzled with sauce after it comes out of the oven."

"Perfect." She smiles at me, and I tap to add it to my order. I add my favorite calzone, along with one of their family-size salads and an order of the garlic knots. You can't go wrong with anything from this place's menu, but especially the garlic knots.

"Dinner should be here around six," I tell her as I put my phone back down.

"Well, that was easy," she tells me as she picks up her phone and smiles at whatever it is she's reading on the screen. "What did you do?" She shoots me a questioning glance.

"No idea?"

"I don't believe you." She swipes up on her phone and reads something. I truly don't know what she's curious about.

"What did I do?"

"According to Avery, she has at least five people interested in more information on meals from me."

"Damn, they work fast! Hell yes, you do."

"I'm still not sure about this idea of yours."

"Why not, it sounds like there is a market for it. Even if you were to only offer it to my teammates' families to start with."

"I'll think about it," she finally agrees. "Avery is asking for a sample menu. She's suggesting I offer four to six meal options weekly, portioned or with four servings each and allowing people to order for a few days, then deliver everything on a set day each week. That way, I can have time to shop for everything after the order deadline and have a few days to cook and portion everything out."

"Sounds like a good way to do things. Then you aren't cooking every day."

"I guess so. It will just make the days I am, long."

"Send her the list of things you made this week and have planned for the next few days, see what she thinks of them," I suggest.

She thinks about it for a few seconds before starting to tap away at her phone. "Okay, menu sent."

"I can already vouch for everything you've made and can only imagine that they'd all love it just as much."

"I'd have no idea how to price out something like this. I mean, I have to cover the ingredients, but also my time. Then, there's the wear and tear on your kitchen."

"Don't worry about my kitchen. I've hardly used it since moving in."

"It looks like there is a kitchen supply company not far from here, maybe I can go check it out and see what their prices are for the packaging containers. Being oven safe will probably make them pricey."

"Maybe so. Do they make them reusable? If you have a small number of clients, maybe you can offer a disposable option for one cost and reusable for another? Give them the choice on how they want things packaged and the cost that goes with it."

"That's an idea. I'm not sure exactly what is available since I've never thought of doing something like this. I just enjoy cooking but have never been formally trained or anything like that."

"Not all cooks have to go to culinary school," I tell her.

"I know, but I also don't want people to think I'm a fraud."

"I think as long as the food tastes good and you are using what you say you are, people won't care."

She just shrugs her shoulders and keeps scrolling on her phone.

CHAPTER 12
KENDRA

6 weeks later

WITH TRISTAN'S SUGGESTION AND ENCOURAGEMENT, I went headfirst into starting my own business. The excitement of setting things up quickly became over-whelming, but a few pep talks from both Avery and Tori, along with my first five orders, calmed my nerves enough to plan out the first four weeks of meals that I'd offer up. I started with four options, for now, with plans to up that to six if things go well.

A knock at the door pulls me from laying out containers on the counter as I start to compile the orders. I head for the door, opening it to find a smiling Avery on the other side.

"Hey! I'm here to help, so what can I do?" she asks, a huge smile on her face.

"Oh, um, I was just pulling everything out to get orders ready for pick up," I tell her as I welcome her into the condo.

"Sounds easy enough. I bet we can get it done in no time at all."

She follows me into the kitchen, taking in all the containers spread out on the long island. "I've got each meal in a different spot. My plan was to gather them together in these," I say as I hold up the reusable bags I purchased that will keep the meals cold for transport. Since this is my first week of actually delivering orders, it's all new. It took me a little bit to get everything I needed ordered and ready to go. I've spent the last few weeks perfecting large batch cooking, as well. I spend two full days cooking two meals each day. I've put crockpots and instant pots to good use in helping me be able to dump and go. I've only had one meal go completely off the rails and have to be tossed out. Other than that, I've been learning more about how to properly measure out a serving and how to package things so they reheat safely.

"Do you have a printed order sheet?" Avery asks.

"I do!" I tell her as I grab my clipboard. "If you want to read off the order, I can grab them and hand them to you to add to the bags, if that works for you?"

"Perfect," Avery says as she reaches for the clipboard. She looks over the sheet, taking in how I've organized everything. "This is amazing, so easy to follow," she praises me.

She starts with the first line, rattling off the meals as I hand them over. Since I've limited my orders to five families, we're able to quickly get all of them packaged up. I add a little thank you card to each bag that I pre-filled-out earlier today. I also include the menu for next week. I printed them on some card stock and cut them out, making them into cute little sheets. It was an idea I found on Pinterest and only took a few minutes to do. I'm sure, eventually, I'll move to have everything listed online, but for now, this personal touch feels nice.

"I'm so excited to try one of our meals tonight!" Avery exclaims once we're all done. She ordered one of each from this week's menu.

"Thank you, I'm excited to hear how you like it. And thanks for the help today, I appreciate it."

"Of course! It was fun and was a good excuse to get out of the house for a little bit."

"I understand that. I have to remind myself to leave here every few days. I think the longest I'm gone is my big grocery store run and my doctor's appointment."

"How's everything going?" she asks.

"Last check-up was great. The doctor has no concerns, baby looks healthy, and I'm right where she wants me to be."

"That's great. Have you heard anything about what's happening back home with your ex?"

"I got a call this week from the DA; he finally took a plea deal, so I don't have to go back and testify, so that is a huge relief. I asked him what I need to do about the baby, and he suggested a few things. Either ask him to sign over his parental rights before the baby even comes or, if that doesn't work, I'll have to take it to court. He said courts don't usually strip a parent's rights easily, so asking for that from the beginning probably won't go well, but I can for sure file for sole custody. With him in jail, visitation isn't going to be an option for a while, so he doesn't see how they'd grant any, for the time being."

"Well, that's a start. Do you think he'd willingly give up his rights?"

"I have no idea. I can't imagine he'd want to be on the hook for child support, not that I'd get much from him even if he is ordered to pay something."

"I know it can't be easy to be in your situation, but do you think it's worth at least asking him? I'm guessing the less you have to deal with him, the better?"

"Oh trust me, if I never have to see his face again, I'd be ecstatic."

"I have a friend that's a damn good attorney. If you'd like me to text her to see if she can draw up some paperwork to have sent to him, I'm happy to do so."

"Really? I wasn't even sure where to start with this mess."

"Absolutely. She's a shark when it comes to protecting innocent kids."

"It doesn't hurt for me to talk to her, so send me her info or go ahead and give her mine. For all I know, I have to hire someone back in Boston to deal with it since that is where he is."

"That I don't know about, but Lucy will be able to answer your questions, though, and I'm sure, if necessary, refer you to someone there that can help you."

"Sounds good."

"Did you ever figure out the insurance stuff?" Avery asks.

"Ugh, no. I was denied for the maternity Medicaid

because they say I have to include Tristan's income, even though we're not together. I get it, I'm sure people try and lie to get it by not claiming everyone they live with, but when we're nothing more than roommates, how is that fair to me?"

"That does suck. The lease didn't work?" she asks.

"I guess not. I got the final decision this week. So now I've got to start researching buying an individual plan."

"It's too bad Tristan can't add you as a dependent on his. The team's insurance is amazing."

"He can only add dependents or a spouse," I tell her. He asked the same question a few weeks ago, but since I'm neither, it's a moot point.

"You could always get married for legal purposes. Then, file for an annulment later, unless y'all finally wake up to your mutual attraction."

"That's never happening. He's just being nice to me because my brother is his best friend."

"Keep telling yourself that if it helps you sleep at night. But from my point of view, that man can't take his eyes off of you. He can find you from across a crowded room in a matter of seconds. I've seen him do it with my own eyes."

"We're friends; close friends, but nothing more."

"If you say so," she sing-songs, but drops it when we hear the door open.

"Hey, ladies," Tristan says, smiling at both of us. "Looks like you've been busy." He points to the orders that are all packaged up on the table and ready for pick up anytime now.

"I figured she could use some help for the first week," Avery tells him. "But even without my help, she would have been just fine with how organized everything was."

"I wasn't worried," Tristan tells Avery. "I watched as she meticulously scheduled everything out, organized it all, and figured out the best way to put it into her order spreadsheet."

"Stop making fun of me, I'm right here," I butt in.

"Not making fun, just pointing out how on top of everything you are. If you weren't so organized, you wouldn't have been so successful right out of the gate," Tristan tells me, his eyes going soft when they meet mine. His gaze causes butterflies to flutter in my stomach and my core clenches with desire.

"Thanks," I whisper. I hold back tears at their praise. Without both of them encouraging me these past few weeks, I don't think I could have gotten this far. But it feels damn good to be here.

Avery stuck around until all the orders were picked up. I gave a one-hour window, and thankfully, everyone stuck to it today. They all loved the packaging I went with. It's only been a few hours since she left, and I've already gotten two text messages with orders for next week, along with a request to take on more orders. Apparently, word is getting around the team and more families want in on my services. I agree to take on two more for next week, seeing how smooth this week went.

Hopefully, I'm not taking on too much too soon, but only time will tell.

"How does it feel to be done with your first drop?" Tristan asks once we're both spread out on the couch after dinner. My belly has finally started to pop out and I'm feeling the effects of being pregnant. Well into my second trimester, I'm noticing so many changes, some on a daily basis.

"So good! Everyone texted saying how much their families loved what they made tonight, so that has been awesome."

"I told you they would," he says as he grabs my feet to start rubbing. He's done this a few times in the past couple of weeks. I try and take breaks, since I have to stand so much in the kitchen while I'm cooking.

"Hmmm," I moan as he hits a particularly tender spot.

"Hmmm good or hmmm bad?" he asks as he presses into the spot.

"Both?" I wince. "I know the pain will bring relief, so don't stop."

Tristan chuckles. "Okay, let me know if I need to let up at all."

I don't say another word, just relax and let him bring me pleasure by rubbing my feet. If how good he is with his hands on my feet is any indication of how good he is with his hands elsewhere on a woman's body, whoever he ends up in bed with is one lucky woman.

"You okay?" his gruff voice asks, and my eyes fly

open. It's then I notice he's watching me as he rubs my foot.

"Yeah," I try and say, but the dryness of my throat makes it come out like a croak. I clear my throat and try again, "Yeah, was just enjoying the massage."

"Just making sure," he says, as his eyes focus on my lips.

I pull my foot from his grasp and stand up quickly. "Thanks for the massage, I'm going to call it a night," I say as I gather my water bottle and the bowl I had some fruit in.

I can feel his eyes as they bore into my back while I practically run away. Maybe Avery wasn't so wrong about her assumption that there is something brewing between me and Tristan.

CHAPTER 13
TRISTAN

I watch like a fucking coward as Kendra runs to her room. Why can't I just man up and ask her for more? I know she wants it; I can tell by the flash of lust in her eyes. Fuck, maybe that's all that it is, lust.

I let my head fall back on the couch and blow out a huge breath. I've been taking my aggression out in the gym and on the ice. It doesn't take much to set me off on the ice, which isn't my normal, and my teammates have taken notice, calling me on my shit every chance they can.

I force myself to stay on the couch for another hour, getting pulled into a documentary on TV. I was afraid if I got up any sooner, I'd go after Kendra, and I don't want to force anything between the two of us. She's been forced enough in life to do things she didn't want to do, I'm not about to add to that list.

Once the show ends, I turn everything off, stopping in the kitchen to make sure the dishwasher is on. It isn't, so I add in the soap and hit the start button before

I head for my room. A sound stops me in my tracks just outside Kendra's door. I lean closer, trying to figure out what I'm hearing. *"Yes, yes, yes,"* she moans. My cock jumps in my shorts, knowing exactly what that sound is. The buzz of a sex toy and the moans of a woman pleasuring herself. I grip my cock over my shorts, giving it a tight squeeze to hold off any further swelling. As bad of an idea as this is, I quietly press my ear to her door, wanting to witness any ounce of her pleasure that I can. *"Fuck,"* she moans again. It almost sounds like she's covering her face with something to dampen her pleasure. It takes every ounce of my willpower to not bust this door down and take over, showing her what real pleasure is. *"Tristan."* She cries out my name and I stumble back from the door.

With my name on her lips as she found her pleasure, I head straight for my room, no longer able to hold back from finding my own release. I drop my shorts and boxers the second my door clicks shut. My palm grips my cock as I shuttle my hand up and down my shaft. The few drops of pre-cum act as the only lubricant until I can make my way to my nightstand and pull out the bottle of lube I keep close by. I put a few drops of it into my palm, allowing my hand to slide up and down my length with ease. I lay back on my bed, tugging my T-shirt off and tossing it aside as I kick back and get comfortable. Visions of what Kendra must have looked like pleasuring herself behind closed doors play like a video behind my eyelids. I stroke harder and faster, wishing like hell that it was her body bringing me to orgasm.

It doesn't take long before I can't hold back the tingle in my balls, and I unload all over my abs. My cock goes limp as I lay there, cum pooled on my skin. My breathing is labored but kicks up when I hear a noise outside my door. Did she hear me outside her own door and come to investigate? Did she hear what I just did, all while thinking about what she was just doing?

I lay there in silence, doing my best not to make a noise. Eventually, I hear footsteps and then the click of her bedroom door closing, and once again, I'm left feeling like a fucking coward.

I'M UP AND OUT OF THE HOUSE THE NEXT MORNING BEFORE Kendra is out of bed. I left a note on the kitchen counter letting her know I had an early appointment with one of the trainers. It wasn't the full truth, I have a standing appointment, but it isn't as early as I played it off to be.

I need to get my head wrapped around what I heard last night and what I want to do about it.

"Are you ready for me?" David, one of the sports therapy interns, asks as he finds me in the weight room after practice.

"Yep, I've been feeling some tightness throughout my hips, so if we can focus on them, that'd be great," I tell him as we make it to one of the treatment rooms.

A perk of being a professional athlete is the access to top-notch medical care all the time. I lay down on the table and he gets to work stretching my body out, along with using some massage to help relax the muscles that are giving me some issues the last few days. I think I tweaked something during a game that I took a hard hit in.

"How's that feel?" he asks when we finish up.

"Better. I'll ice and maybe we can do this again before tomorrow's game?"

"Of course. I'll mark you down for pre-game treatment. Does just after morning skate work for you?" he asks as he checks the schedule.

"Yeah, I'll probably come skate for a short amount of time, so that works."

"I've got you down, see you then," he says before letting me go. I don't want to push myself into an injury, so I hit the showers so I can get out of here.

I'm about to pull out of the parking lot of the rink when my phone rings, Jackson's name flashing on my dash.

"Hey, man," I greet as I connect the call.

"What's up? Haven't heard from you in a while," he reminds me.

"Sorry, just been busy between games and practices," I tell him.

"I caught your last game. What was that fucker saying to you before you laid him out?"

"Just running his mouth, kept trying to take cheap shots on everyone, so I put him in his place," I say. Some of that is the truth, but not all of the truth. I also laid into him to get some of the pent up energy I have built up out. The energy that I'd like to channel into sex with Kendra.

That thought brings her to the forefront of my mind. The way she looks standing in my kitchen, all sexy in her yoga pants and tank tops. I swear, the ones she has were painted onto her body, showing off every dip and curve her body has to show. The way her body has started to change as it fills out during her pregnancy has me wondering if I have some pregnant woman kink I didn't know about.

"You still there, man?" he asks, bringing me back to the present.

"Yeah, must have been a bad spot, lost you for a second," I lie.

"How's Kendra doing? She tells me everything is going well."

"As far as I know, everything is great. She sent out her first set of orders yesterday and already had more orders by the time she went to bed last night," I tell him proudly. "She said she even agreed to take on a few more orders for next week."

"That's awesome. I'm glad she's found something she enjoys."

"I'm just glad she isn't out there working for some asshole boss. This way, she can take it easy when she needs to. I also don't mind the added benefit of my fridge always being stocked with meals," I tell him.

"I'm sure you don't," he chuckles. "I need to get back to work, I just wanted to check in. Don't be such a stranger."

"I'll do my best. You know how focused I get some-times during the season, but I'll try a little harder," I promise my best friend.

"Talk to you later, man," he says before the line goes dead. I feel like such a fraud. Like I'm hiding something earth shattering from him. The way I want his sister on such a deep level feels like I'm betraying him.

I walk into the condo and find Kendra at the table, the laptop I bought her a few weeks ago open and her eyes scanning the screen.

"Hey," she greets, not looking away from it.

"Hey, how's it going?" I ask. By the look of things, something is wrong. Her brows are pulled together, and it looks like she's been crying.

"I got denied for the maternal insurance coverage, so I've been trying to find another option and everything I find is out of my price range," she says, tears welling at the corners of her eyes.

"Let's get married. I can put you on mine," I blurt out, and she looks at me like I've grown a second head.

"You can't be serious," she says.

"Why not? It isn't like I'm dating anyone. We can keep it a secret, if you want. It will just be a legal thing. Go down to the courthouse, sign a few documents, and then I can add you on within days. No one has to know about it other than those that process the paperwork."

"Isn't that fraud?"

"Maybe, but who's going to ask?"

"I don't know, but what if we get caught?"

"If we legally get married, then I take that marriage license to my employer and add you onto my insurance, no fraud has been committed. If someone wanted to come search this condo, you live here. Your stuff is here, and it is obviously not just stored here. You run your business out of the kitchen for even more proof that our lives are intertwined."

"We have different bedrooms," she says, her eyes meeting mine from over the top of her computer.

"That's easy enough to remedy." I smirk, flashing her my trademark panty-melting smile that has gotten me laid more times than I can count.

Kendra just rolls her eyes at me. "I'm sure you wouldn't want me warming your bed and messing with your lifestyle."

"Sweetheart, you have no idea what you're talking about. And when was the last time you saw me bring home another woman?" I challenge.

"Um, none that I'm aware of since I got here," she admits.

"Exactly. I haven't been with someone else since before I flew to Boston," I tell her, watching her eyes widen at my honesty.

"No hotel hookups? Since August?" she questions, obviously not really believing what I've told her.

"No one. The last time I was with a woman was the night before Jackson called me. Two of them, actually." I figure if I'm being honest with her, I might as well lay all my cards out on the table.

Her nose scrunches up at my honesty.

"Threesomes not your thing?" I ask, and wince at the way she attempts to make herself smaller in the chair. "Shit, I didn't mean anything with that question."

"No, it's okay. I just remember there being three guys that night, what I don't quite remember is how many of them forced themselves on me," she says quietly.

"Fucking bastards," I curse.

"They're in the past," she says as she stands and comes in front of me. "I'm only looking forward, thanks to you." Kendra pushes up on her toes and places a kiss on my cheek. "Thank you for being my savior. I don't know what I'd do without you right now. Can I think about your suggestion for the next few days and then let you know? Maybe once you get back from the weekend road trip?"

I cup her cheek, enjoying the feeling of her skin against mine as she leans into the touch. "Take whatever time you need," I say, my voice gruff, the longing I have for her getting harder and harder to hide.

"Thank you," she says, never breaking eye contact with me. It takes all my willpower not to lower my lips to hers, taking them in a kiss I so desperately want.

"Are you coming to the game tomorrow night?" I finally ask, breaking the trance we're both fighting.

"That was the plan. Avery offered to swing by and pick me up when she leaves for the game. I think we're going to just grab some dinner once we get there."

I can't help but smile, knowing that she'll be at my game. It isn't the first one that she's attended this season, but for some reason, it feels different.

I HIT THE ICE, MY LEGS FEELING GOOD AFTER MY treatment this morning, and then a good nap this afternoon. I wasn't sure how I'd sleep today as my previous game-day naps have been hit or miss with Kendra living with me now. I'm usually so amped up when I get back on game days that I can't fall asleep before my alarm is going off again to get back to the rink on time.

I make a few laps, scanning the faces to see if I can find her. I know she was getting dinner with Avery beforehand, so they might not be here yet, or at least in their seats.

I drop to the ice, going through my normal warmup routine. Stretching out my body, my legs especially, to help keep from injuring myself.

"You ready to kick Tampa's ass?" Ryker asks as he stops next to me.

"Hell yes, I'm feeling at least one goal tonight," I tell him, and hope like hell I can deliver on that prediction.

"That's the type of confidence I like to hear." He taps me on the shoulder. "I need you to have that more often."

"Trying, man, I really am."

"I know you are," he tells me before his attention is drawn up to the stands. I turn my head to see what he's looking at, when my eyes land on his daughter, wife, and Kendra. I about choke on my own tongue as I take her in. Standing there in a jersey. *My jersey.*

Getting an erection with a protection cup on isn't something I've ever wanted to experience , but right now, my cock has other ideas.

She must notice me looking at her as she gives me a little wave and I nod my head in acknowledgment before I break away from Ryker and take a few more laps around our half of the ice. I need this ache in my balls to go away or else I won't be playing at all tonight. Thankfully, after my first run through our shooting drills, my cock has gotten the memo that right now isn't his time to shine. It's work time and he can come out to play later.

We hit the locker room after warm ups, Coach comes in and gives his last-minute pep talk, along with reminders of what the other team is excelling at lately. What players we need to keep a man on at all times, and how the defense—my department—needs to protect our goalie, Blake, tonight. Tampa has some snipers on their team that will take any opening we give them.

The alarm sounds, letting us know we've got two minutes until the starting lineup is announced to the packed arena. I love the production our team makes to pump up not only the crowd but also us players. We really do feed off of the fans' excitement some nights.

With the ceremonial stuff done, and the anthem sung, the stadium lights are all on and the refs are ready to drop the puck and get this game going. I line up in my assigned spot, waiting patiently for our center, Jason Soaps, to win the face-off and pass the puck back to one of us D men.

He cleanly wins the draw, dropping the puck to my defense partner, Damien. He quickly gathers the puck and heads for the zone, which we cleanly enter on-sides. He passes the puck up to Ryker, who looks for the shot, but doesn't have a clear path to the net, so he passes it back along the boards behind the net and swings it over to Aiden, who taps it up to me on the blue line. I settle the puck on my stick and swing with all my might, sending the puck flying toward the net as it sails just over the shoulder pad of the Tampa goalie. The ref blows his whistle, signaling the goal just as the goal horn blows and the crowd goes wild. My teammates all crash into me, celebrating our early lead.

Once we're done celebrating, we make our way over to the bench, accepting a line of fist bumps from all the guys. "Fucking amazing start," Aiden calls out as we make our way back into position at center ice for the face-off.

The game continues at that high energy I felt in the first minute. Three more guys add to our lead before the first period is over, sending us into the first break in a nice spot, up four nothing.

The next two periods were still fun, but Tampa swapped out their goalie and he was able to limit us to just two more goals the rest of the game. We still pulled out the shutout, with a six to nothing final.

"Who's going out celebrating tonight?" one of the guys calls out once we all make it into the locker room after the game ended. I finished my night with the one goal and three assists, which earned me the second star of the night.

"I'm out, sorry," I call out to the room. As fun as going out with my teammates can be, there's only one place I want to be tonight, and that's at home with Kendra. The idea of her in my jersey hasn't been far from my mind.

Most of the married guys also decline the offer to go

out, which I don't blame them. We're leaving tomorrow for a road trip, so they want to spend as much time with their family before being gone for a few nights.

I get through my post-game interviews as quickly as I can, then hit the showers and get dressed in my suit so I can get out of here as quickly as possible. I check my cell for any missed texts or calls, seeing a text from Jackson, one from Kendra, and another from my parents.

> **JACKSON**
>
> Shit man, you are on fire tonight. Keep it up!

His text makes me chuckle and, looking at the time stamp, he most likely sent it shortly after I scored that first goal, thirty seconds into the game.

> **KENDRA**
>
> Avery is taking me home, see you when you get there, I'll try and stay awake until you do.

I figured she'd go home as soon as the game ended, Avery often doesn't hang around for Ryker. She's got early mornings with her job, as well as the fact that Ellie has school in the morning that she needs to get home and into bed for.

> **DAD**
>
> Nice game son, you looked good out there tonight. Call when you can, we miss you.

I smile at my dad's text. He's always short and to

the point. His text is a reminder that I've slacked on calling them every few days to check in like I normally do. I've been a little busy and pre-occupied lately, so hopefully they understand. But I also make a mental note to call them sometime tomorrow to catch up.

I snag my suit jacket from the hook in my stall and toss it over my shoulder. "Night," I call out to the locker room, which is met with echoes of the same sentiment. Everyone is busy doing their own thing, just trying to get out of here as quickly as possible.

I make my way to my car in the secured players' lot. I'm always careful when leaving, as sometimes fans will line up outside the gates, hoping to spot a player and have them stop to sign something quick. Thankfully, tonight, it doesn't look like anyone is doing that in the dark. I head straight home, making it there in just over twenty minutes, thanks to traffic.

I'm quiet when I enter the condo, only the glow of a lamp comes from the living room and the soft hum of the TV turned down really low.

I enter the living room and take in a sleeping Kendra on the couch, curled up with a throw she added to my couch for when she's cold. She's so peaceful hugging that blanket and the pillow to her chest. I hate the idea of waking her up, but I also know she'll get much better sleep in a bed than on the couch.

I decide to go and change out of my suit before waking her. I want to be comfortable if I end up needing to carry her to bed.

When I come back out from my bedroom, she's still sleeping soundly on the couch. I click the lamp off and approach her, deciding if it's better to just scoop her sleeping body up into my arms, or if I should wake her up and offer to help her to bed, first. My need to hold her close wins out, so I slide my hands under her body, carefully lifting her into my arms. I have to get her firmly in my arms before she wakes up, a little startled to find herself in my arms, but she settles quickly, wrapping her arms around my neck as she rests her head on my shoulder and relaxes into me. "Are you taking me to bed?" she asks sleepily.

"Yes, you need good sleep," I tell her softly as I walk to her room. I push the door open with my leg and walk her to the bed. I attempt to pull back the covers while still holding her. It isn't as easy as I thought it would be, but I manage to get them partially out of the way so I can lay her down. Once she is lying on the bed, I scan her body to see what she's wearing. She's still in the pants and jersey she wore to the game tonight. I have no clue if either are appropriate to sleep in, so I shake her lightly. "Kendra," I call her name, a little above a whisper. "You need to wake up for a second, baby."

Her eyes flutter open and she takes me in, hovering over her as she sleeps on her bed. "You're in bed and need to wake up so you can change, maybe use the bathroom before you fall asleep for the night," I tell her. It takes her a few seconds to process my words, but she finally does and starts tugging at the jersey as she sits up.

I can't find words as she tugs it over her head. I wasn't sure what I'd find on her underneath it, but I see that she was fully layered up. She pulls the long-sleeved top off, exposing her creamy skin and a bra that is having trouble holding her ample tits into the cups. I bite back a groan. What I wouldn't give to suck her nipples into my mouth, caressing them with my tongue as I tease and build up her release.

I force myself to look away, as the longer I look, the harder my cock swells in my shorts, and they do nothing to hide my response to seeing her strip down.

"Can you hand me that T-shirt?" Kendra asks, pointing toward the chair by the window that has some clothes tossed onto it. I snag the oversized shirt and hand it over, attempting to be a gentleman and not gawk at her once again.

"Do you need anything else before I crawl in bed and call it a night?" I ask once she's tugged the T-shirt over her head. She has a hand tucked up underneath it until she pulls it out, along with the bra she was just wearing.

"I think I'm good, thank you, though."

"Anytime," I tell her before I practically run out of her room and into my own. I close and lock the door immediately, then turn and lean back on it as I sink to the floor. My cock is straining hard, wanting to be let out of the cage it is currently locked away in. I sit here and will my body to relax. It's got a mind of its own, so I finally push back up and stalk for my bathroom. Another shower it is. I angle the shower head to spray a little harder on the wall in order to clean up the mess I'm certain to make when I unleash this load.

CHAPTER 14
KENDRA

THOUGHTS OF THE OTHER NIGHT KEEP PLAYING IN THE back of my mind. Tristan carrying me to bed. Tristan standing close by as I stripped out of my clothes and handing me pajamas. His cock straining in his shorts, not hiding the effect our closeness had on him.

I've been thankful to have a few days reprieve without him here. We've texted a handful of times each day he's been gone on this trip. I found myself turning his game on and watching from home as I worked on my grocery list for next week's food orders. I have a spreadsheet that I can plug in exactly how many orders I have of a specific meal, and it tells me what I need to fill said order. I do this for each meal that is on the menu. I tried to group like minded meals together. Ones that allow me to make one thing but use it in multiple ways.

I finalize my list, happy with the way things are working out with this new adventure I'm on. I set my list aside, I'll tackle it all tomorrow when it's officially shopping day for the week. Now that Tristan's game is finished, I hit the button and turn the TV off. My mind is a little bit on overdrive between the game and working on my list.

I'm startled when my phone rings, my brother's contact flashing on the screen. I immediately accept his call, putting him on speaker so I can relax back into the couch.

"Hey, big bro," I greet.

"Hey, how's it going?"

"Can't complain, I just finished making my shopping list for tomorrow."

"How's the business going?"

"Seeing how it will be my second week, it's good," I chuckle. "Everyone was super happy with my meals, and returned with orders for this week, along with a couple more people."

"That's awesome, Kens, I'm so fucking proud of you. How's living with my lug of a best friend?" he asks, and I'm glad that he can't see me right now, as I can feel myself heat with a blush.

"It's fine, nothing to complain about. He's clean, doesn't sit around scratching his balls and leaving messes everywhere for me to clean up," I tell him, my mind wandering back to Chad and his ways.

"He'd better not be, I'd have to fly out there and kick his ass," he says and I can tell he's joking, but also serious at the same time.

"I have a question for you. I need you to keep an open mind and listen to everything I have to say before you interject," I blurt out.

"Okay…" He draws out the word, obviously intrigued.

"A little background to what my actual question is. After I got here, I applied for the state insurance for pregnant women. They denied me, so I appealed the decision with a made-up lease from Tristan, as they were trying to say I had to include his income and therefore don't qualify. Even though I'm just staying here, they still didn't care and said all income has to be included. I'm kind of screwed without getting that approval. I can't afford the personal plans, especially if I'm going to save anything to start affording baby items. Tristan asked if he can just add me to his policy, and he can, but we'd have to get married, first." I take in a deep breath, shocked I just blurted all of that out at once. Jackson is still quiet, and I'm not quite sure if he's still on the other end of the line. "Are you still there?" I ask, a little nervous.

"Yeah, I'm here," he confirms.

"Okay, just wanted to make sure. Before he left, he suggested that we should go down to the courthouse and get married. Get the paperwork that would allow him to add me to his plan, then later, we can have it annulled and no one would be the wiser. Do you think I'm stupid for contemplating this idea?"

I can hear Jackson blow out a huge breath in his silence. "Part of me says he's a genius for thinking of it, and part of me says hell no. What would that look like? He's not known for his commitment to one woman, what is he going to do, keep it in his pants for months on end?"

"I-I don't really know how we'd deal with that kind of stuff. I think he was under the impression that we could keep it under wraps we'd even gone out and done it. Basically, only tell those that need to know. The fewer people who know, the better, and the less we have to confess to when it's all over."

"But at what point is it over, you're always going to need insurance. The baby is going to need insurance."

"I don't really know. It was kind of something he tossed out on a whim, but it had enough merit I've been thinking about it. I told him I'd try and have an answer for him when he got back."

"I think, I guess I don't really know what I think," Jackson laughs. "If this is something you want to do, then you need to go into it with your eyes wide open and some ground rules in place. Have things spelled out on how you're going to handle legalities, the annulment, hell, even things like the birth certificate. I know some states automatically put the husband's name on it if you are married, even if you know for sure that person isn't the biological father, so you might check into that."

"I had no idea. And that might become a sticky situation. If the baby isn't Tristan's, which it obviously isn't, can he or she even be on the insurance once they're born? God, I have so much to think about and figure out. I told him this all seemed like fraud."

"In a way it kind of is, but it isn't like they're requiring a DNA test," Jackson points out.

"I just don't know what to do," I tell my brother, doing my best to hold back the tears that want to fall.

"As long as he doesn't put his hands on you, I don't care what goes on."

"That's not very helpful," I groan to my brother, but am just met with his laughter. "Enough about my problems, right now, how are you doing?"

"Good, I went on a date last night," he tells me and I perk up.

"Really? And? What's her name?" I spit out questions.

"Her name's Gabby, well, Gabriella Kane," he says, like I know who that is.

"Okay, was she nice, how did you meet her?" I ask.

"She was very nice; we've got a second date set up for later this week. You've met her, actually," he says, but doesn't elaborate.

"Not ringing a bell," I start to say, then stop. "Did you say Kane, like, Dr. Kane?"

"I did," he says, and I can tell he's smiling.

"How did that come about?" I ask.

"She left those business cards, and I texted her once with a question right after you were released. That led to her following up to see how you were doing and, well, we just never really stopped texting over the following few weeks. I finally asked her out on a date, and we just clicked. Neither one of us was ready for the night to end, but she had early morning rounds she had to get to this morning."

"Wow, well, I hope it all works out. What I remember of her, she was really nice. Seemed sweet."

"Yeah." He sighs and I'm sure if I could see him, he'd have little cartoon hearts floating above his head.

"It's been a whirlwind of excitement, that's for sure. Never thought anything good could have come out of your hospital stay."

"I'm glad something good came from it." I smile slightly, not really sure what to say to that, but also happy that my brother is happy. He deserves it.

"So back to your predicament, what do you think you're going to do?" he asks.

I blow out a breath, stalling as I mull over the million-dollar question. "I don't know. I'm truly at odds over the whole situation."

"Go with your gut, that's my best advice."

"You won't be mad at either of us, right?" I ask, not wanting anything to come between Jackson and Tristan.

"What is there for me to be mad about? It isn't like the two of you will be in a real relationship," he states. All I can think of is the obvious attraction lingering between Tristan and me. What if something was to take form and grow between us, and I'm not just talking about my baby bump.

"And if something did?" I ask for clarification.

"Is there something you aren't telling me?" His voice grows defensive and demanding.

"Not really," I say, frustrated that I'm fucking this conversation up. "I think it's the pregnancy hormones or maybe the white knight-like feelings I have for Tristan, but it just seems like there's something different between us."

"Or maybe that teenage crush you always had and tried to hide?" Jackson asks.

"You knew about that?" I groan.

"It wasn't hard to see, Kendra." He laughs at my expense. "You were always trying to be all up in our business when he was around. Took every chance you could to walk around in your bikini or made sure to sit right next to him when we'd be on the couch watching movies or TV."

"I was thirteen with raging hormones, it isn't like you didn't do the same damn things around some of my girlfriends."

"Touché," he admits. "To be honest, I'm not really sure what to think about the idea of the two of you becoming a real couple. I'm not going to say it can't happen, because that's not for me to say. The two of you are grown ass adults who can make decisions, all I'm going to say is be careful. You've been through some shit, and I know he'd never treat you like that asshole ex of yours did, but he's also used to a different life-style, and I'd hate to see either one of you get hurt. I'd also really fucking hate to have to beat my best friend up because he broke my sister's heart."

"You're the best big brother, I hope you know that, Jackson," I tell him sincerely. "I love you."

"Love you, too, sis. I just want to see you happy."

"That means the world to me, thank you," I whisper, as I've apparently lost my voice thanks to the emotions boiling up inside me.

"Do I need to keep this conversation under wraps if and when I talk to him?" he asks.

"Um, maybe for now. We'd discussed not telling anyone about the marriage option, so I don't want to catch him off guard if you were to bring it up before I can tell him that I talked to you about it."

"All right, just let me know when that's happened so I don't slip up."

"Will do."

"Call me in a few days, let me know how things are going," Jackson states more than asks.

"I can do that," I tell him before we finish up our call. I clean up the small mess I made from dinner tonight, along with the papers I printed out to go over all the orders placed this week. Not only did I take on the extra clients, but a few families also ordered larger quantities of some meals. As tiring as the shopping, prep, and cooking days can be, I'm excited to have this opportunity.

CHAPTER 15
TRISTAN

I toss my gloves to one of the equipment managers as we make our way off the ice. We fell to Buffalo three – two in regulation. I'm having a hard time not taking responsibility for the loss, seeing as how they scored their third goal while I sat in the box for a minor penalty with under two minutes to play. It fucking sucks, but it is what it is.

"Don't beat yourself up over that call," Ryker says to me as we enter the visitors' locker room. It isn't anything fancy, visitor ones usually aren't. Just a U-shaped room with spots for each of us. The goalies have their own section, both goalies requiring more space than the rest of us due to the size of their gear. I always thought my bag was big growing up, until I made friends with a few of the goalies.

"Was a piece of shit call," I tell him, and he nods his agreement.

"I won't argue with you on that."

"Not your fault, man," Blake, our goalie tells me as

he walks past. "I should have had that puck in my pads. I still don't know how it tricked through." He shakes his head side to side.

"You wouldn't have had to face it had I kept my ass out of the box and on the ice," I tell him.

"Let's leave it in the past. Look forward to the next game. We need to get out there and win those two points," he tells me and we bump fists. If there's anything I've learned from this team of guys it's how important it is to look forward and not dwell on the past. We can learn from our experiences and past, but we need to leave it all behind us and move forward to grow.

I sit down in my stall, taking a moment to rest. I shake up the blender bottle one of the training staff left for me with a protein shake ready to go. They make sure all of us have adequate nutrition when we come off the ice, whether that's after a practice, game-day morning skate, or after a hard fought game. Once I finish the drink, I start stripping all my gear off. The equipment managers collect everything, making sure it is all dried off or cleaned. It is their job to pack everything up and get it to the next place.

My rookie season in the NHL, I made the mistake of packing my own bag before the first trip. The equipment manager of my team had to unpack and re-pack it the exact way he liked things to be done so that he could verify that I didn't forget anything (spoiler alert, I'd missed one of my elbow pads), but also he packed it a very specific way so that everything would fit how he wanted it to for traveling.

Once I'm showered and dressed, I make my way to the motor coach that is waiting outside the back entrance for us. It will take us directly back to the airport so we can fly out and back home. I find myself excited to return home, and it isn't because I'll get to sleep in my bed again. It's because I'm excited to see Kendra. I realize I miss seeing her every day when I'm gone.

It's the middle of the night when we land back in California. Everyone is tired from the half-sleep we get on the flight, so we're quick to say our goodbyes and head out. Thankfully, we have the day off, so I can sleep in and get in a little downtime to help recover from the jet lag that comes with playing on the other side of the country.

I slip my key into the lock, turning it slowly so it stays quiet. I don't want to wake Kendra up on acci-dent. When I slip into the condo, a sweet smell fills my nostrils. She must have been baking something again. The smell makes my stomach growl as I think back to how delicious the cookies were she made a few weeks ago. I could definitely go for another dozen or so of those.

I push my suitcase down the hall, stopping for a second outside of Kendra's door to listen for any signs she might be awake. I'm met with silence, so I continue into my bedroom. I strip out of my suit, hanging it over a chair so it doesn't wrinkle before I take the time to hang it back up. Since I'm home for the next week and a half, I need to get a stack of my suits taken to the dry cleaners. Maybe I can get that taken care of after I've slept for the next few hours.

I must fall asleep quickly as the next thing I know, the sun is coming through the cracks in my curtains as the smell of something cooking wafts in under my door. My stomach growls once again, reminding me of when I got home last night. I roll out of bed, feeling pretty good after yesterday's game and the flight home. I take a quick shower, then pull on some joggers and a team T-shirt. I just need to take care of a few errands today, so comfortable and casual is all I need.

I head for the kitchen, needing some coffee and breakfast, stat. I find Kendra in her element, scooping some kind of batter into muffin tins. "Something smells amazing, what are you making?"

She smiles up at me, a little flour or something on her cheek. "Blueberry muffins, would you like one? I have a batch that is cooling already."

My mouth waters at eating another one of her baked goods. "Absolutely. Do you happen to have any coffee brewing?" I ask before rounding the island and entering the kitchen.

"Yep, should still be plenty hot," she says and nods toward the pot. I grab a mug and fill it up to the very top, lifting it to my lips as I take my first sip. The hot liquid feels divine going down, the jolt of caffeine hitting me almost instantly.

I lean back on the counter opposite where Kendra is filling the muffin tins, watching her as I drink my coffee. She looks back at me when she's finished, giving me that smile of hers again. I love how comfortable she's become in my home. Having her here with me feels natural, like this is where we both belong. The strange thing is, those thoughts don't scare me. With my coffee finished, I set the cup on the counter and reach for one of the muffins.

I remove the wrapper and take a large bite, taking about half of it all at once. "Damn," I mutter around a mouthful. "This is incredible."

"Thank you, I used a new recipe I found online; I'm glad they passed your taste test. I was going to offer a free half dozen with each of my orders this week to see if anyone would be interested in some easy grab-and-go breakfast items."

"Something is wrong with the customer if these don't seal the deal for additional orders from them," I tell her.

"We'll see," she muses. "How was your trip? Sorry about the loss."

"Did you watch it?" I ask.

"I had it on. I was working on my orders but watched most of it."

"I mean, it sucks we lost, especially since I put my team down a player when Buffalo scored the game-winning goal, but it is what it is. We can't win every game, and at least it wasn't a blowout."

"You looked pissed about that call."

"It was such bullshit. He exaggerated the trip so much, should have been an embellishment call on him, but that wasn't the way the cookie crumbled last night."

"They can call that?" she asks.

"Oh absolutely. Some guys will way overdo it to try

and get a call against the other team. I've seen it called plenty and is usually really warranted."

"So besides the bullshit call, how was the trip?"

I can't help but smile at her cursing. I don't know why it makes me smile, but it just does. Maybe it's the fact I've known Kendra since she was a little girl, and I remember how shy she was back then. Always the rule follower. The innocent one.

"It wasn't bad. Short ones aren't usually that bad. It was just a strange one since we went all the way to the East Coast for only one game. We usually go for a handful since it is the farthest we travel. Add in the time zone changes, it can be a bitch on the body to make all the changes."

"I was wondering why you guys were going all that way for only the one game."

"Just how the schedule worked out. There is a lot that goes into making the schedule and I wouldn't want to be the one in charge of that."

Kendra places the last tray of muffins into the oven, then gets to cleaning up her mess. I try to help, but she kicks me out to the other side of the island. I take a seat on one of the bar stools, not wanting to lose her company. We fall into a conversation. She tells me all about her spreadsheet and the shopping she needs to get done today. I offer to go and help, be the muscle for carrying all the heavy bags so she doesn't wear herself out. She hesitated, but finally agreed to my offer and is letting me help.

Once the muffins are out of the oven and cooling,

she heads off to change before gathering her shopping list and we head out for our first stop.

I'm impressed with how organized she is. She's got everything broken down by what store and in a way that she only has to make one pass through each section. If I were in charge of this excursion, we'd be making a mess of this, zig-zagging back and forth around the entire place multiple times.

It takes us a few hours to get everything, but we've finished and are in my SUV and ready to head home. "How about we order some lunch, I've worked up quite an appetite after all that shopping," I suggest.

"Yes, I'm starving."

"Any requests?" I ask as we sit in the parking spot.

"Do you know of any places around here that have really good clam chowder? I haven't had any and it is really making me miss home," she says.

"I do, actually." I pull out of the parking spot and head for the restaurant.

Since we had a trunk and back seat filled with all of Kendra's groceries for the week, we take our lunch to-go, heading back to the condo.

I use one of the carts the building has to help get everything up to my place in the least number of trips. I like knowing they have these available for her to use, especially as she gets later into her pregnancy and I'm not always going to be around on the days she needs to shop to help. Once everything is upstairs and the refrigerated stuff is at least put away, we both sit down to dig in to our lunch.

"So how'd I do with the chowder?" People from

Massachusetts can be snobs when it comes to our chowder, well, any seafood, really, but San Francisco is also pretty known for it, as well.

"So good. I don't think I could even make it this good," she says between bites. We opted for the bread bowls, but the restaurant bagged those separately and gave us containers of the soup so the bread wouldn't soak up all the liquid before we got home and make a mess.

"I tried quite a few places last year until I found one that reminded me of home," I tell her.

We are pretty quiet as we both finish, but I can tell she's got something to say, if the way she's squirming has anything to do with it.

"Everything okay?" I finally ask once I'm finished eating.

She pushes her own plate away, and I don't miss the way her hands shake slightly. She bites the corner of her lip, as her eyes meet my own. "I think we should get married," Kendra blurts out.

"Okay," I say, nodding in agreement.

"But I think we need to set some ground rules, first."

"Ground rules?" I ask, scratching at my cheek, rolling her words around my mind. "Like what?"

"I talked to Jackson about our idea," she says, and I cringe at what he thinks about it. "He was actually okay with it, also, side note, did you know he went on a date with one of the doctors that saw me?" she asks.

"He did?" I ask.

"Yeah, the OBGYN that came in the one day. I guess they started texting, mostly about me, at first, and then that blossomed into more. Sounds like they really like one another."

"Good for them. Now, back to the ground rules," I redirect, not wanting to lose focus on the important things. I can call Jackson later and bust his balls for not telling me about his dating the doctor himself.

"While I was talking to him, we discussed so many things that we need to take into consideration. Things like the birth certificate. Some states will automatically put the husband's name on it, even if he's not the biological father. I'd never ask you to take responsibility for my child, so we need to figure that out. Then, there comes the issue of will the insurance allow the baby on the insurance since you aren't its father. Once we figure all that out, we need to decide on an end date. We can't continue this charade forever, so an end date would be good to know before it even starts," she says, stopping only to take a breath before continuing on. "How secretive are we going to keep it? I'm not convinced some tabloid isn't going to see your name on the public records and leak the story that you got married, so it might be better for you to release the information so we can control it. That also leads into the more personal things, like us not being caught with anyone else in compromising positions."

"Contrary to popular belief, I can keep it in my pants." I smirk at her. "I've done it this long," I remind her.

"Yeah, but that's a lot to ask of you to do for another year or so."

I think about that, and she's right. Another year

without sex will fucking suck. But then another idea hits me.

"If we're going to be legally married, nothing says we can't take advantage of all the perks." I bounce my eyebrows at her and love it when she cracks a smile and a laugh falls from her lips.

"You might think that now, but I doubt you'll be saying that when I've got a big belly in the way."

"You're beautiful now and you'll be beautiful then," I tell her honestly.

"Won't sex blur the lines between us?" she asks.

"Not if we both go into it knowing that we're just using one another, for the time being," I insist.

"I don't know that I could do that without catching feelings."

"I get it, it isn't for everyone. Just a suggestion so we're both not sexually frustrated. You can only do so much to pleasure yourself," I say, and can't forget the sounds I've heard coming from the other side of her bedroom door. My cock swells in my boxers, ready to take care of that itch for her anytime she wants. I also don't miss the blush that creeps up her cheeks, probably at the memories of how she pleasures herself.

"Have you ever thought of me while pleasuring yourself?" she asks, and I'm caught off guard by her straightforwardness.

"Would it change your view of me if I said yes?" I ask.

"I don't know," she says, biting that lip again. "Just mostly curious."

I lean forward so I'm closer to her. "I've thought of

no one except you since you got here," I tell her honestly, my voice not hiding my desire for her. "Especially the night I heard you making yourself come with a vibrator. If I'm not mistaken, I think I heard my name fall from your lips when you came, so I think it's safe to say we both have used each other already."

She gasps, her eyes hooded at my words. She licks her lips, and I can't stop the momentum as my lips crash into hers. I'm tentative, at first, letting Kendra warm up to the idea. I let her make the first move to deepen the kiss. As soon as she does, I take control back, cupping her cheeks as I angle her just the way I need her so I can devour her mouth. I somehow stand without breaking our kiss, pulling her up at the same time so I can sweep her into my arms. I kiss her like my life depends on it. My erection pulses as it's entrapped behind my clothes, but feels good nestled against her belly.

I break the kiss, resting my forehead against hers, and suck in a deep breath. "Let me make you feel good," I plead. "I promise you won't regret it."

She keeps her eyes on me. I can tell she's debating my words behind those eyes. "Please don't hurt me," she whispers, and my heart fucking cracks in two. I can't even fathom doing one thing to hurt her, and hate the man that did.

"Never," I tell her before I place a kiss on her forehead. I link our fingers together before I lead her to my bedroom. I have this incredible desire to have her spread out in my bed. I stop when we're next to the bed, cupping her cheek as we stand toe-to-toe. "Any doubts and you say the word, and we stop. I don't care when that is," I tell her. "You're in the driver's seat."

Kendra nods her understanding. I reach down and grip the hem of her shirt. I slowly slip it up her body. She lifts her arms, helping me as I pull it over her head. My eyes fall down to her supple tits. The ones I got a good look of the other night when I helped her to bed. I drop a hand to her collarbone, tracing my fingers down the exposed skin, loving the response her body is giving me as it breaks out into goose bumps at my touch.

I slowly lower my hand, tracing over the swell of her breasts. I bend my knees, lowering my head as I place kisses to the flesh while I flick the clasp of her bra open and tug the fabric out of my way. I suck a nipple into my mouth, toying with the bud as it hardens under my touch. The moans that fall from Kendra's lips egg me on, telling me she's enjoying this just as much as I am. I switch to the other side, showing attention to the one my mouth just left with my hand. Kendra drags her fingers through my hair, the scrape of her nails on my skin sends shivers down my spine and into my balls.

I pop her breast out of my mouth, moving right back up to capture her lips with mine. I wrap an arm around her back and take us both down onto the mattress. My entire form covers hers, but I need more, I need to feel her naked body against my own. I break the kiss, standing back up so I can strip us both bare.

I tug her yoga pants down, exposing her small baby bump. It's amazing to see the changes her body has made these last few weeks. From the bruised and broken state she was in when I arrived at the hospital, to now. All her outwardly bruises are healed, and she appears to be doing okay, most of the time. The thought does hit me that it might be hard for her to be intimate with someone else, so I need to keep that in mind as we move forward, right now.

"Are we still good?" I ask as I tug my own clothes off.

"Yes." She nods, letting me know she's good.

I let my pants fall but leave my boxers. "Like what you see, sweetheart?" I ask as she takes in my body and licks her lips.

"Mhmm," she hums, "I'd like it more if you dropped the boxers, let me see it all, since you've seen all of me."

"You're perfect," I remind her as I brush my thumb over her clit. My fingers sink into her folds, her wetness coating them, and my cock twitches again. I give him a tight squeeze as he needs to learn to wait his fucking turn. I can't withhold any pleasure from her, so I tug the boxers off my hips and let them fall to the floor. I give my cock a few good tugs as she watches me, her eyes widening at the sight.

"Um, that's not going to fit," she says, looking again at my cock. I know I'm a little bigger than average, but I've never had the issue of it not fitting. It just takes a little bit of foreplay to get my partner really ready.

"I've got you, sweetheart, by the time I'm done with you, you'll be able to take every inch."

"I'm not so sure." She squirms under my watch.

"Is that you saying we're done here?" I ask, not wanting to pressure her one bit.

"I don't know," she says, biting her lip. "I'm just scared it will hurt."

I hover over her, bring my lips down, and press a kiss to the corner of her mouth, move them down her jaw line and then to her neck. "Let me try, if it hurts, we stop. I promise to only bring you pleasure. "

I wait for her response. The way she arches into me and attempts to rub her center against my cock tells me she wants this more than she doesn't. "I need your words, sweetheart," I insist.

"Yes," she finally says.

I kiss her deeply as I run my fingers back down her body. I circle her clit, but don't press directly onto it. Making her want the contact. I slip two fingers inside her body, loving the way her center engulfs them, squeezing them tightly as I pump in and out, fucking her with my fingers.

"Let go, let your body just feel," I whisper against her skin.

"So close," she pants as I increase my movements. I can't help but smile at her telling me that, like I can't feel the way her body is responding to my touch. The way her pussy tightens with each stroke of my fingers. I can only imagine how it's going to feel stretched around my cock when we're to that point. I need her nice and relaxed before I slide inside her with my cock. I'll plan to make her come a few times before that happens, and hopefully, I don't embarrass myself by coming on the first thrust when I do finally slide in.

"Give it to me, sweetheart," I coax as I slide down her body. I bring my lips to her center, my fingers still working her as I suck her clit hard. She explodes, my fingers coated in her release. I lap at her, drinking it all in as she thrashes against my face. I can't get enough as she goes limp against the bed.

I kiss her inner thighs, letting her body relax and enjoy the endorphins that an intense orgasm brings.

I slide back up the bed, lying on my side facing her as she takes all the time she needs to recover. I slowly stroke my cock, keeping him happy while waiting until it is his turn for pleasure.

"That almost looks painful," Kendra says, looking down at the head of my cock.

"It isn't," I tell her as I kiss her cheek. "Just looks that way, I promise. How are you feeling?"

"So relaxed." Kendra rolls onto her side toward me. We're lying just inches apart, our breaths mingling as we stare at one another.

"Good, are you ready for another one?" I ask as I tuck a lock of hair behind her ear.

"Another one?" she asks, her brows furrowing.

"I promised you pleasure, I plan on delivering that promise." I kiss her lips. "My definition is at least three orgasms." I smirk. I know it's a bit cocky, but what can I say, I like sex, and orgasms are the ultimate goal.

"That's a bit lofty of a goal, don't you think?"

"You should always have a goal to reach for, otherwise, how else do you measure your accomplishments?" I ask.

Kendra shrugs her shoulders. "Good point." She laughs.

I drape a hand over her hip, gripping her ass cheek

as I pull her until our bodies are completely touching. "If you haven't noticed, I'm quite fond of you and this sexy body. I think a few more orgasms are just what we both need."

I swallow her words with a deep kiss before I get to work on that second and third orgasm, making good on my promise.

CHAPTER 16
KENDRA

MY BODY TINGLES FROM THE SECOND ORGASM THAT Tristan has wrung from my body. I never knew being intimate with someone could be this liberating. The way he worships my body, the way he's made my pleasure the priority before his own. He's refused to let me help him along, saying that his pleasure will come later.

"I told you it would happen." He kisses my shoulder. "Just took the right coaxing with my tongue." He's so cocky, but I guess when he's got a mouth like that, he's allowed to be cocky.

"Yeah, I'm never leaving this bed," I tell him as my eyes flutter shut. It takes a few moments for my words to hit my head and I worry for a moment he'll take them wrong.

"Good, I rather like you here," he says, his lips still against my skin.

We lay wrapped in one another for a little while, my body loose like a noodle that's been cooked. "Stay right here, I'm going to grab a condom," Tristan says.

"You know I can't get pregnant again," I say as he rolls away from me. I instantly miss the heat of his body.

"I know how biology works." He laughs as I hear the drawer next to the bed open, then the crinkle of a foil-wrapped condom. "I've just never gone without. Not ready for that yet," he tells me honestly.

I roll over and watch as he rolls the condom down his length. I'm still not sure about him fitting, although he says I will. "Where do you want me?" I ask.

"I should be the one asking you that." He smirks and gives his cock a few strokes. "I don't want to hurt you, tell me what will be best."

"I don't really know," I tell him honestly. "Can we try missionary, then move to something else if that isn't working?"

"Anything you want," he says as he crawls back to me. He hovers over me, my legs falling open to accommodate his body. He's had his face down in my most intimate areas, but there's just something about this moment that has me nervous. "Look at me," he instructs. "What's your safe word?" he asks.

"Pineapple," I blurt, no idea where that word came from.

"Alright," he laughs, "all you have to say is pineapple and I stop, immediately. Understand?"

"Yes," I say as clearly and with as much conviction as I can.

Tristan reaches down and slides his fingers through my folds, then grabs his cock and does the same with his tip. It feels so good but also leaves me wanting so much more. He lines his tip up with my entrance and slowly pushes forward. His cock slips inside, my body easily stretching around his cock until he comes to a stop, our bodies fully flush.

"God damn, you feel so good," he groans, just before his mouth takes mine in a deep kiss. His tongue duels with mine as he pulls back and thrusts into me, each thrust building in speed and strength. My body is already so relaxed it doesn't take long for my orgasm to build up. I can't believe I have another one in me, but the way he plays me, it does exactly what he wants it to.

"So close, don't stop," I pant as we break our kiss. My nails scrape into his back as I hold on for dear life as his thrusts become a little wild. The sounds of our bodies slapping together as we both chase our releases.

"I'm close, sweetheart, I need you there," he says as I feel his cock swell. That added pressure on my g-spot sends me over the edge as I grip his cock like a vise and cry out. The most epic orgasm that I've ever had in my twenty-four years of life race through my body as I let go. My orgasm must set Tristan over the edge as he slams into me one last time. He's loud as he calls out in pleasure, his sweaty body resting against mine. He's careful not to crush me, although I enjoy the weight of his body holding mine down.

He eventually catches his breath and pulls from my body. I hate the feeling of emptiness. "Come here," he instructs as he pulls me with him while he rolls onto his back with me tucked into his side.

I go willingly, wrapping my body around his, never wanting this feeling of intimacy to go away, but knowing that it isn't mine to keep with Tristan. This idea that we can be intimate and not grow feelings isn't going to work. I know that because I've already caught feelings for him.

I PULL OUT TWO CROCKPOTS, GETTING THEM SET UP ON THE counter so I can get moving this morning. I'm admittedly moving a little slower than normal after spending half of yesterday and then all night in Tristan's bed with him. We had sex again before we fell asleep, that time a little slower as we were both tired.

I pull out the veggies I need to chop, adding them to the crockpots for the pot roast I'm making for one of this weeks' meals. Once I have everything for those going, I pull out the instant pot and add in the chicken and spices for shredded chicken. I have two meals this will be become. I love how versatile it is. Once that is cooking, I get the soup started on the stovetop.

It takes me a few hours, but I'm finally able to sit down for my first break of the day. As soon as I'm on the couch, my feet up, as they are starting to bother me, my mind wanders to the last twenty-four hours. The care that Tristan takes with me makes me wish for so much more with him. I don't know why he doesn't think he's the settling down kind of man. He shows me such a tender side of him I truly believe he could be that man for me, but I also don't want to be the type of woman who thinks that I can change him. I'd never want him to resent me for anything, especially changing who he is if it isn't something that he wants.

I must doze off, as I wake up when I feel a set of lips against my own. "Afternoon, sweetheart," Tristan greets, a sweet smile tugging at his lips.

"Hi," I say, stretching as I wake up. "What time is it?"

"A little after two," he tells me as I sit up. "What time did you sit down?"

"Like twelve thirty or so," I tell him.

"Didn't get enough sleep last night?" He quirks a brow, a shit-eating grin on his face.

"Someone kept me up past my bedtime." I swat at his chest. "Kept trying to do naughty things to my body."

"Nothing you didn't like." He smirks back.

"I didn't say that, did I?" I ask as I kiss him.

"No," he admits. "Have you had lunch?"

"I haven't. I was planning on some after I sat down for a little bit, but apparently I fell asleep before I could get back up."

"Good, let's go find something together. I'm starving."

"I need to check on my meals and then I can make us some sandwiches, maybe sneak a few bowls of soup out of the pot on the stove," I tell him.

"Sure, that sounds good."

I head for the kitchen, checking on both crockpots. They are both coming along but have a few more hours until the pot roasts will be nice and tender. The chicken from the instant pot was done before I rested, as it didn't take long to cook. Now, I just have to separate it out for the shredded chicken tacos and creamy chicken and rice dish that I'll be using it for.

I stir the soup; it has been simmering for the last few hours and is looking perfect. I ladle some into two small bowls, then make us some sandwiches to go with the soup.

"Let me help you with that," Tristan says as he sees me attempting to balance both bowls and plates to take to the table.

He grabs the one I hand him, and I follow him to the table. We eat in silence, both hungry due to the late hour to be eating lunch.

"How was practice today?" I ask once we're both done.

"Pretty normal, spent a little extra time getting stretched out after I got off the ice."

"Do you do that a lot?" I ask.

"Just depends on how my body is feeling. I put my body to work yesterday, needed a little recovery from it." He winks at me.

"You're so bad," I laugh at him.

"Like you didn't enjoy it?" He raises an eyebrow at me.

"I didn't say that. I think you're just playing up the effect it had on your body. If anyone should be sore today, it is me," I tell him.

"And are you?" he asks, a little concern lacing his voice.

"Maybe a little, but not where I'd have thought I'd be," I tell him. "After standing all morning in the kitchen, my feet and legs were killing me. I think I'm going to have to get some uber-sexy compression socks for all the time I spend standing."

"Would some of those cushy kitchen mats help?" he asks.

"Probably. I hadn't really put much thought into it," I tell him.

"Get whatever you need, you don't want to start swelling, if you can help it. I can't imagine that would be good for you or the baby."

I squint my eyes at him. For a bachelor who wants people to believe that he's allergic to relationships, he surprises me sometimes with little tidbits of knowledge he has regarding pregnancy or babies.

"It can be a sign of things, but some swelling is normal for pregnant women."

"I know, I read about it," he states matter of factly.

"You were reading about pregnancy?" I ask, a little shocked.

"Yeah, I bought an eBook and have been reading it when traveling."

"Color me shocked," I tell him. "Why?"

"I figured it would be a good thing for me to know what to expect, that way, if you needed my help, I'd have a little clue as to what you were going through."

"Your teddy bear side is showing again," I tease him.

Tristan just shrugs his shoulders in response. "I'd feel like an asshole if something was wrong, and I didn't know it."

"You're one of a kind, don't let anyone tell you

differently." I stand so I can give him a hug. His thoughtfulness about brings tears to my eyes.

"Only for you," he says into my side. I run my fingers through his hair as I look down at him, the way his eyes dance with desire has my core clenching as I remember just how good he felt there last night.

"I need to get the soup divided up," I say so I can step away, needing a little distance between us so I don't go jumping him right here in the dining room.

CHAPTER 17
TRISTAN

I'VE LOOKED UP ALL THE LAWS FOR GETTING MARRIED. California actually offers a confidential license. Thanks to the number of celebrities that live here and might want to keep that kind of information private, it just costs a few extra bucks to apply for that type of license. I knew that was one of the things Kendra was worried about, so that takes a little stress off her shoulders.

It's Thursday, so pick-up day for her orders. I love that she's found something she loves and can do from the comfort of the condo. I try and stay out of her way, knowing that she's got a system in place, and she doesn't need me to get in the way.

I get home from practice, finding Avery and Tori both here helping Kendra as she packs up orders. I can't help but smile at how quickly they brought her right into their circle and made her feel welcome.

"Hey, Tristan," Avery says when I enter. "Is my husband with you?" she asks.

"Nope, he was still at the rink when I took off."

I haven't even finished my sentence when the buzzer is going off, alerting that someone is here and wanting to be buzzed in. "How much do you want to guess that is him?" she laughs.

I press the button. "Hello."

"Let me up, asshole." Ryker laughs into the speaker.

"Who you calling an asshole?" I chuckle before I hit the button.

"Told you," Avery smirks. "He knew I was here helping Kendra and he said he couldn't wait until I got home to see me," she says. He is so far gone for his wife it isn't even funny.

I sit back and enjoy the company of my friends. It doesn't take long for Aiden to also show up, since his wife is here. What I expected to be a somewhat quiet afternoon, turns into a fun one with everyone.

※

IT IS FINALLY JUST KENDRA AND ME. I'VE GOT ALL MY research to catch her up on, so I've been looking forward to everyone going home and all her orders being picked up.

"I've done a little research," I start to say.

"About what?" she asks and mutes the TV so she can give me her full attention.

"Marriage license laws," I tell her, and can see the surprise that I've taken the lead in this. I know she told me that she thinks we should move forward with my offer, but then we got distracted by sex, and well, someone needed to do something about it.

"Go ahead," she says hesitantly.

I do just that, filling her in on everything I found out. It is actually a pretty straightforward process, we just need to go down together to apply, pay the fee and sign a document, and they'll issue it right on the spot, then we have up to ninety days to make it legal. We can do that a few different ways, and I go over all those details.

"Sounds easy enough," she says.

"I thought so, too, and we can go with the confidential one for a little added protection."

"Probably not a bad idea. Do you think it would still be a good idea for your agent to make an announcement so that if someone leaks it, he's on top of it?"

"I can run it by him, but even if it is leaked, what are people going to say, other than I got married?"

"I've seen how they dig and dig on other celebrities' spouses. I'd rather people not be digging up my past," she says, and I can tell that part of all this is bothering her.

"I promise to do whatever I can to shelter you from that, but I can't promise no one will figure out who you are and what's happened in your past," I tell her honestly. I tug her closer to me on the couch, needing to touch her and provide whatever comfort I can.

"I know, it just still seems like such an elaborate idea that is going to backfire."

"We don't have to do it," I remind her.

"One minute, I think it's the only answer, and the next, I think it's the worst idea we've had in all of this." She motions between the two of us.

I turn her so she's facing me. I don't want there to be any misinterpretation of my next statement. "I'll never regret my time with you. I wouldn't offer you any of this if I didn't want to."

"Thank you," she whispers. "I appreciate that more than you can ever know. So are we really going to do this?"

"I say we do it." I kiss her lips.

"Okay," she agrees, a smile breaking out on her face. "When?"

"That depends on how quickly you want to get it done, and when we can get an appointment at the license office."

"I can look it up and then we can decide, because if the next appointment is weeks away, then there is no reason to try and rush and make it happen."

"Then, look it up," I suggest. I wait patiently as she grabs the iPad on the counter and looks up the information.

"It looks like there are some random spots open as soon as early next week, and they open up more as the week progresses, or going into the following week it is still pretty open," she says as she looks at the screen.

"Is that just for the license, or can we also get married there, as well?" I ask. I remember reading that some places offer the officiant, as well, if you want a courthouse wedding.

"This location also offers the service. When is your next day off?" she asks, looking up at me over the iPad.

I check the calendar on my phone. "I have Monday off, then, as long as Coach doesn't change anything,

Thursday will be an optional skate, and Friday morning will be optional morning skate."

"It looks like we could make an appointment for the license Monday morning, but they don't have a ceremony spot that day. If we wanted to do both in the same day, we'd have to push that off until Friday."

"What do you want to do?" I ask, not really caring what option we go with.

"Do you know where this place is located?" she asks, showing me the map with the building flagged.

"It's downtown, looks like not far from the rink."

"So kind of a pain in the ass to get to, then?" she asks.

"Eh, it's not horrible, and I think there are a few parking garages in that area."

"Okay, so what do you think? One trip and get it all done at once, or split trips?"

"How about we do the one, that way, it gives you a little bit of time to make any plans you want for the day," I suggest.

"I don't need anything fancy. It isn't like this is a real wedding." She rolls her eyes at me.

"I didn't know how much we'd need to play it up to not make anyone suspicious," I tell her.

"I didn't think about that, hmmm," she hums. "I guess it wouldn't be a bad idea for me to wear a nice dress and maybe take a small bouquet of flowers. Are we bringing anyone with us as witnesses? It says here we can bring up to six guests, but that they aren't required. The clerk's office will sign all the required documents."

"I guess that depends on if we're telling anyone about it," I state, leaving that decision up to Kendra.

"I don't know, they're your friends. What do you think they'd say?"

"They're your friends, too. True friends will stick beside you no matter what you do, and I don't see them saying anything about our situation. I'd like to think either of them would do the same thing if in the same position."

Kendra chews on her fingernail, her undecidedness glaringly obvious. "It might help make it seem real if we have people there to support us," she finally states.

"Do you want Jackson there?" I ask.

"If this was my one and only wedding, absolutely, but that seems like a long way to come for a fake wedding," she says. "Don't you think?"

The idea that this is fake hits me square in the chest and is like a knife right to the heart that's being twisted. "Yeah," I say, my voice gruff as I try and hide the hurt, or disappointment, or whatever the hell this feeling is that I'm having right now.

"Can we ask Avery, Ryker, Tori, and Aiden to come, then?" she asks.

"If that is who you'd like to be there, then I'll make it happen. What time do they have appointments available on Friday?"

"They have a nine a.m. license appointment and a ten a.m. ceremony appointment. Will that allow you to still get in your game day naps? It says ceremonies are given forty-five minutes for use of the space, but that the actual ceremony is less than ten minutes, including signing all the paperwork."

"Yeah, that should be fine. I don't usually lay down until closer to one."

"Should I go ahead and book it?" she asks, a little excitement obvious in her voice.

"If that's what you want, then let's do it," I tell her, my heart still aching that this is all pretend and not real.

"Is it what you want?" She pauses and really looks at me.

I can't tell her that I have no idea what in the hell has come over me lately, that I'm feeling things I've never felt for a woman, and now I'm almost ready to say we're throwing all the rules out the window because I don't know how I'll let her go when a year is up. "I want whatever you want," I say, doing my best to convince her with my words.

She gives me a stern look and I worry I'm busted with the way I swear she looks past my eyes and into my soul.

"I know you offered to begin with, but if this is something that you've changed your mind about, I'll completely understand. It is a little bit crazy of an idea," she tries to give me the out, but dammit, I'm here and committed to helping her; I'm not backing down, at this point.

"Book the appointment," I state, no mistaking the seriousness of my words.

"Done," she says. "We're getting married!" She smiles sweetly from where she sits.

"Does that mean you'll come to my game that

night?" I ask, wondering if she'll also wear my jersey. My name and number plastered on her back.

"I'd love to," she confirms, and I can't hold back a smile.

"Come here," I state, crooking a finger.

She does as I ask, standing and walking to where I've sat down. She stands in front of me, and I can't hold back from resting my forehead against her little baby bump. I've noticed it start to stick out lately, and she's no longer able to hide it unless she's wearing really baggy clothes. "Hey, little one, I'm marrying your mommy next week, what do you think of that?" I say to her belly, knowing that the baby can't understand me or answer back. The idea of being the father figure in this little one's life is actually something I could see myself looking forward to. It doesn't scare me like I'd thought it would. I want to be here, seeing all the changes that are to come, and watch Kendra turn into the best mother.

CHAPTER 18
KENDRA

"I KNOW THE PERFECT PLACE WE CAN GO LOOK AT dresses," Tori says as we finish up lunch. I finally asked the girls to lunch over the weekend and told them what we're doing, as well as invited them to our fake marriage ceremony. I think the shock has worn off, and now they're on board with helping me prep for the day.

"I say we also plan a spa day on Thursday, get manicures and pedicures. I can come over the morning of and do your hair and makeup, if you'd like," Avery suggests.

"That will make for a really early morning, are you sure?" I ask.

"There is a hotel right across the street from the clerk's office. We could get a room for Thursday night, that would cut out the commute time in the morning and give you a place to get ready. You might even have time to go back to the room between appointments," Avery adds.

"That's an idea. I was worried about it being down-town and the traffic," I admit.

"Let's do it, then," Tori says. "Done, I booked their two-bedroom suite, so we'll have plenty of room."

"Damn you ladies are fast," I chuckle. They've known of my plans for less than an hour and have already made decisions for me.

"Give us something to plan, and we're all over it," Avery laughs.

"And I just booked my favorite makeup artist and hair stylist," Tori says as she taps away at the screen on her phone. "Gotta love my connections in the industry," she says, referring to her job at the record label she's some bigwig at. I honestly don't really even know what she does for them, I just know she knows a shit ton of famous singers and does something with them.

"I don't know if we need a professional, plus, that sounds expensive," I tell her, not really sure how I'd afford something like that. Tristan and I didn't really discuss spending money on this. I mean, he knew I was going shopping for a dress today. He insisted I put it on his credit card and that I wasn't to look at the price tag, I was to buy whatever one I wanted. I don't think I could ever do that, spending a huge amount on this fake wedding seems like a waste of money, so I'm trying to do it as cheaply as possible.

"Don't you worry your little mind about that, it's my treat," Tori insists.

I give her the world's longest side-eye, but cave to her insistence when she side-eyes me right back.

"Can I get you ladies anything else?" the server asks as he comes back around.

"I think we're good, just the check, please," Tori answers for us.

"Of course, I'll be right back," he says before stepping away from the table. I reach for my wallet, ready to pull out some cash to cover my portion of lunch.

"Put your money away, it is no good around me," Avery says.

I try and object but realize I'm fighting a losing battle.

We leave the restaurant and head inside the mall to the store Tori told us about. They have some beautiful dresses; most are fancier than I need. I talk to the sales lady, and she says she has some perfect options for me.

I head for the dressing room where she said she'd meet me. I sit down on the chair and wait. She enters a few minutes later with four dresses on hangers and in bags. She starts to remove them, all so beautiful.

"Does one of these call to you more than the others?" she asks.

I look at all of them, reaching out to touch the material to see if I get that feeling.

"I really like this one," I tell her, pointing to the second one. It's got a lacy layer overtop a solid white stretchy material, perfect for going over my bump. It has three-quarter sleeves, and a V neck, so keeps things classy.

"Perfect, let's get you into it and see how you like it on," she suggests. "I'll step out and let you change, just speak up if you need any help. This one doesn't have any zippers, so you're good to go on that front."

She steps out of the dressing room, so I undress, pull the dress over my head, and then adjust the stretchy layer, then the lacy overlay. The dress hugs my curves, showing off my bump. It seems so big when cradled in something tight like this. I've been wearing larger, baggy clothes most of the time, so I don't realize just how big it is getting already. Time sure is flying by lately.

"Oh, you're gorgeous," Tori gasps when I walk out to the viewing area where both women sit.

"I agree. How do you feel in that option?" Avery asks me.

"My bump looks huge," I tell her as I rub it. I've found myself doing that a lot lately. That and talking to it like my kid can understand.

"I think it looks perfect," the sales lady states.

"I do really like it," I say as I turn on the little box they have so brides can see the entire dress if trying on a long one. This one stops just at my knee.

"Do you want to try on any of the others, just to compare?" the sales lady asks.

"I think it would be worth it since we're here," Avery encourages.

"Okay, let's try option two," I agree.

I try on all four options, always coming back to the first one as my favorite. Once we've eliminated the other three, we move on to some shoes. I know with the swelling I've been having, high heels are out of the picture. Thankfully, the store has a few flat options. I fall in love with a simple sandal hat will look great with the dress but also be something I can pair with other outfits, and they won't be too dressy.

I hand over Tristan's credit card after I've picked out all the things, cringing when it's time for the total. It isn't as bad as I was thinking it would be, so that makes me feel slightly better about spending his money.

"I can't believe that was so easy," Avery says as she links her arm through one of mine as we left the store. "Tristan is going to swallow his tongue when he sees you on Friday," she adds.

"No, he isn't," I insist. I decided not to tell them about us sleeping together. I wasn't ready to share that part of our arrangement.

"I know you don't see it, but the way that man looks at you, whew." She pretends to fan herself with her free hand. "That boy doesn't hide his feelings for you very well. I'm surprised you haven't noticed it," she questions. I'm thankful we're walking and not looking at one another because I'm not sure I could hide the truth. I'm sure it is written all over my face that we're not holding back our want for one another, at least the sexual want.

"I think you're seeing things," I try and insist.

"Don't be so quick to disregard what Avery has said. I also noticed a difference in Tristan. He's different with you, and I don't think it's just in a 'you're his best friend's little sister, she's family' kind of way. He watches you from wherever he is in the room. The game you came to and wore his jersey, I saw the moment he saw you for the first time, and I swear on everything that is holy, if you weren't already pregnant, he would have made sure that night you got pregnant. It was like you put on a target and were his prey."

"I-I don't even know how to respond to that, but I can assure you, nothing happened between us that night."

"That night," Avery asks, "does that mean something has happened between the two of you on another night?"

I hate lying to people, so I stall, trying to figure out how to get out of this without making a huge mess of things.

"We had a moment, but that was all it was." I try and play it off cool, like he hasn't made me come so many times I've lost count.

"Okay, I get it. You want to keep all the juicy details to yourself. We're here for you when you're ready to dish. And what is shared on girls' day, night, anytime, stays between us girls. You have our word on that," Tori says, stopping in her tracks to make sure I can look at her and see how serious she is about that.

"Thank you, I appreciate that," I admit. It is nice to have some girlfriends who want what is best for me and are looking out for me.

"We like you, and think you're good for Tristan. If the way he's changed since you arrived is because of you, then we're all for it," Avery adds. "It's just a bonus for us that you are a bomb-ass cook and are an even better person and want to be our friend."

"You sure know how to make a girl cry," I tell them

both as I wipe at my eyes. "These damn pregnancy hormones have me crying at the drop of a hat."

"Girl, I cried once because there were only two Oreos left in the package and I wanted four. I made Aiden go to the store at almost midnight to get me another package. He thought I was crazy, but still did it and loved every minute when I thanked him after he returned."

"I'm sure he did," I laugh.

"Hey, pregnancy hormones made me horny all the fucking time. I couldn't get enough dick. It was torture when he was gone on road trips. I wore his ass out when he was home."

"I thought something was wrong," I admit. "I had to go buy some extra batteries to have on hand."

"Yes, my vibrator got a good workout in when he was gone. Just be careful that Tristan doesn't bust you with that thing. You might not be able to hold him back." Tori winks.

"That would be so embarrassing, don't jinx me," I tell her, hoping that she hasn't done just that.

"Oh come on, you know real dick is so much better than any orgasms that you can give yourself. And I'm here to tell you that once your belly gets bigger, there will come a day that you can't do it anymore."

"I might cry when that day arrives," I admit.

"Once again, I'm sure Tristan will be more than willing to be your special helper," Tori states, and I have no clue how she doesn't crack a smile.

"Alright, enough about pregnancy sex and hormones, I need your attention and focus for later this week," Avery says as we take a seat at a table in the food court of the mall. "I'm booking us appointments starting at three o'clock on Thursday afternoon. Massage, followed by a quick facial, then pedicures and manicures. Anything else you'd like for your pamper appointment?" she asks me over the top of her phone.

"Ummm, not that I can think of," I tell her, as I've never been to a spa before.

"Tori, anything else?" she asks her best friend.

"Sounds good to me, are you booking at the hotel's spa?" she asks.

"Yeah, figured that was easiest with us staying there."

"It's a great spa, I've been a few times. Then, we can plan on dinner at the steakhouse upstairs after all that, or if we want something a little more relaxing, they can bring the food up to the room for us. What is your preference?" Tori asks me.

"I don't really have an opinion," I admit. "I'm happy with whatever is easiest."

"I kind of like the idea of ordering room service. That way, we don't have to feel like we must get all gussied up after relaxing at the spa just to go eat dinner. We can stay in lounge clothes in the room and just relax," Avery suggests.

"Done. I'll add it to our room preference," Tori states.

"You can tell Tristan to meet you at the hotel. We'll snap a few pictures of the two of you before you head out. Do you want us to come along to the license appointment or just for the ceremony?" Avery asks.

"Um, I don't really have a preference," I tell them.

"We can come and get more pictures. I know you say this is all fake, but I want you to have something to remember it by when you both wake up in a few months and realize that it isn't quite so fake," Tori says.

I can't argue with her, and she knows it.

With a plan in place for the rest of the week, we walk around the mall a little longer. I window shop while Avery and Tori both buy a few things. I can't stop from checking out all the baby clothes in a few of the stores. It all looks so small. I haven't started buying anything yet. I want to wait until my ultrasound before I get anything.

Once we've had enough, I head back home, an air of excitement hovering over me as I look to my future, one that temporarily ties me to Tristan, of all people.

I get home, taking my dress straight into my room and hanging it up in the closet.

"Did you have a successful trip?" Tristan asks when I join him in the living room.

"Yep, got a dress and shoes to go with it. The girls booked a spa day for Thursday, along with a hotel for that night for the three of us. It's right across the street from the clerk's office, so I'll have extra time to get ready. They want you to come there to pick me up."

"Okay, I can do that," he says, like what I just told him isn't overkill for this fake wedding.

"Tori also booked one of the hair and makeup artists she knows from her job," I tell him, not sure what he'll think of that.

"Having friends with connections has perks." He

smirks. "I bet you'll look beautiful, not that you aren't always, but you know what I mean," he says, shutting up so he doesn't accidentally offend me. I can't help but laugh at his predicament.

"I know what you mean," I let him off the hook. "I am a little excited, I won't lie. This will be my first time ever going to a spa."

"Really?" he questions.

"Yeah, I've gone to nail places in strip malls for a manicure or pedicure, but never to a spa for a massage or facial or anything like that. Avery booked us for all of that," I tell him.

"I'm going to have to buy her a really nice gift for her next birthday," he muses.

"Why's that?" I ask him.

"Because she's taking care of my girl," he states, like it's the obvious answer. "I'm guessing it is safe for you to do all of that while pregnant?" he asks.

"Yes, she confirmed that they offer a pregnancy massage. Showed me a picture of a special table that accommodates the belly so I'm not putting direct pressure on it when lying face down. Depending on the brand the location has, some have special pillows that you lie on with the belly cutout and other tables have a removable portion that accommodates the belly," I explain from the images we looked at earlier.

"Interesting. You'll have to tell me how you like it, afterward."

"That I can do," I confirm.

"I'm going to move everything forward by one day this week, so I don't have orders going out on Thursday afternoon. I might move them to Thursday morning, but that will kind of depend on when I finish cooking."

"I'm sure your clients will all understand the need to move your normal pick-up window, and if it doesn't work for someone, I can always be here on Thursday afternoon for them to stop by."

"I appreciate that," I tell him.

"You look exhausted, are you feeling okay?" Tristan asks.

"Yeah." I yawn. "Walking around and shopping just made me tired. I think I need to sit down for a little bit." I rub my belly, which I've noticed, lately, seems to be sticking out more. There is no more hiding the fact that I'm pregnant. I'm still wrapping my head around the fact that I'll soon be a mother.

"Come rest." He pats the couch next to where he is sitting. "I can make us some dinner," he offers.

"You don't have to, I can make something in a little bit," I start to offer, but he cuts me off.

"I know you can, but that doesn't mean that you always have to be cooking for me. Let me take care of you for a change."

The look he gives me has me swallowing my words. I guess he's right, I don't always have to be the one that is doing everything. I need to learn to accept other people's, especially Tristan's, help. It is just one of those things that I've become so accustomed to that it will take time to un-learn.

CHAPTER 19
TRISTAN

I STAND IN MY WALK-IN CLOSET, SCANNING THE SUITS THAT line one wall. I don't usually ever have an issue with choosing what suit I'm going to wear each day, yet today I find myself standing here, not sure what one to put on. What does a man wear to his fake wedding?

I grab a solid black one from the hanger. A Tom Ford suit I bought a few years ago when I felt like I'd finally made it in the league. I could justify the high price tag for the immaculate suit. I don't wear it often due to that high price tag, so I think today justifies pulling it out.

With my outfit picked, I head back into the bathroom and trim my beard back down to the small amount of facial hair I tend to keep. I'd let it get a little long this past week. Getting ready makes my mind wander to Kendra and what she must be doing at this hour at the hotel with the girls.

I knew my friends were kick-ass and would pull her right into the fold when she came to stay with me, but they've gone above and beyond, and for that I am forever grateful. She needed the sense of belonging and I hope we have provided that for her.

I splash on a little cologne, then head back into my room to put my suit on. I check myself over in the mirror, then head out. I give myself extra time to make it down to the hotel. You never know with the morning traffic here in the Bay Area.

My palms are sweaty as I leave my keys with the valet. I know this is all for show and ultimately to help Kendra for the next few months, but I can't help but think what if it isn't.

As I walk through the open door of the hotel lobby, my phone rings in my pocket. I pull it out and see Jackson's face flashing.

"Hey, bro," I answer the call.

"Well, any cold feet? Do I need to fly out there and remind you she's my sister?" he asks, trying to make his voice sound stern.

"No and no. I just got to the hotel she stayed at last night with the girls. Our appointment is in about forty-five minutes."

"Okay, well, I'm trusting you with my baby sister. There's no need to consummate the marriage, since it's fake and all," he says and I have to wonder if he suspects anything.

Choking on my own saliva, I smack my chest before I reply. "Fuck, man, I'm not one to kiss and tell, but shouldn't that be between the two of us, if we decided that's part of this arrangement?" I know this is going to rile him up, but I think it is a valid question.

"I'm going to pretend like you didn't just ask

permission to fuck my sister," he growls. Little does he know, I've already done so. The knowledge of that hits me like a ton of bricks and I feel like an asshole friend. But at the same time, I don't regret what has happened between Kendra and me, and in the end, that is all that really matters as long as it is what the two of us want.

"As much as you might object, your permission isn't needed. She's a grown-ass woman who can make her own decisions, and I refuse to let you get in the way of that. Being her brother and my best friend be damned," I say to Jackson.

He must hear the seriousness in my voice, as he just grunts what I'm guessing is his agreement. "Well, good luck today. Send me some pictures so I can see how beautiful she is on her fake wedding day."

"I'm sure she'll bombard you with pictures," I chuckle.

"Probably," he laughs, and I hope that means we're back on good terms.

"We good, man?" I ask, wanting to make sure.

"Yeah," he sighs, "I'm just trying to make sense of everything. Knowing everything she's been through this year, and now this. I know in my soul that you wouldn't do anything to hurt her, but it is still hard to wrap my mind around you settling down and being what she needs. I just didn't take you for the husband and father type."

"I didn't take myself for that, either, but I promise you, I feel like this is what I'm supposed to do like I know I need to take my next breath, or how I know skating on ice fuels my soul."

I can hear him breathing, probably letting my words sink in. "Just take care of her, that's all I can ask," he finally says.

"I promise," I tell him as my phone chimes with an incoming text message. I pull the phone away from my face to look at it and see that Avery is texting, asking where I'm at. "Hey, man, I've got to go, the girls are texting to see where I'm at."

"Good luck, we'll talk later."

"Later," I agree before ending the call and stepping on the elevator.

The ride up takes less than a minute. I walk down the hall to the room number texted to me. Just as I'm about to knock, the door swings open. Avery stands at the door in a nice dress. Past her, I can see a large living space that is void of anyone else. "She's still in the bedroom with the hair and makeup people. She's just glowing, you're going to swallow your tongue," Avery says, a huge grin filling her face.

"Okay, and how do I look?" I ask, sliding my hands down my suit jacket.

"Very nice, perfect choice in suit." Avery winks. "She should be out in just a minute or so. They were just doing some finishing touches after she got into her dress."

"All right, you must be the groom?" A woman I've never seen before comes out of what I assume is the bedroom.

"Guilty," I tell her, looking between this woman and Avery. I notice a camera in her hand and realize she must be a photographer. This must be another idea of Avery or Tori.

"Hi, I'm Chloe, I'll be taking some pictures today. Can I have you come over here, and stand facing this way, please?" She introduces herself and jumps right into what she wants. I follow directions, standing where she wants. Once I'm there, she moves my hands, brushes off the lapels of my jacket. "Perfect!"

I hear the click of the shutter on the camera and realize she's already snapping pictures of me. "All right, Kendra is going to walk out and place her hand on your shoulder, I want you to keep looking at me until I give you the okay to turn around. I want a few shots of the two of you before you get to see her," she tells me. I realize she's probably a seasoned wedding photographer and this is standard. I'm not going to argue, protesting that this is all not necessary. This wedding is just to get us that little paper so I can get Kendra added to my insurance to help make her life a little easier. "Kendra, step just a little closer," she tells her, and I can feel her behind me. "Perfect, now take your hand and place it right here, over Tristan's shoulder, like this," Chloe tells as she shows her. I feel Chloe's hand touch my shoulder before it is replaced by Kendra's.

"Y'all look so cute!" Tori exclaims as she comes around to stand to the side so she isn't in the way, but she can watch what is happening.

"All right, I need both of you to look this way, give me your best smiles," Chloe instructs as she holds her camera up to her face. The click-click-click of the shutter fills the room as she oohs and aahs and moves around, getting a few different angles of the two of us. "We're done with that pose. I'm going to get Kendra how I want her, Tristan, stay put until I say when." She flitters around, and I can tell Kendra has moved away slightly.

"Just a time check, they have fifteen minutes to be at the clerk's office," Avery pipes in.

"This won't take long," Chloe tells her, as she continues to move behind me.

"Tristan, I want you to turn towards your right slowly on the count of three," Chloe says, then starts her count. "One, two, three."

I start to turn, my eyes immediately taking in Kendra as she stands just a few feet from me. She's absolutely gorgeous. The dress she bought is hugging her curves like it was made to fit her like a glove. My dick takes notice and twitches against the zipper in my slacks. "You look gorgeous," I tell Kendra as I close the distance between the two of us. I can't help but reach out and touch her. One hand cups her elbow as the other caresses her cheek.

"Yes, perfect!" Chloe calls out, and it's then that I remember this is all being caught on camera.

"Thank you," she whispers, her eyes never leaving mine.

I want nothing more than to press my lips to hers, but that isn't what this is. Not right now, at least, with the audience we have. I'll get my chance to kiss her when the ceremony is over, then, hopefully, again tonight once we're alone at home.

"We're good for now, I'll get everything else once we're done," Chloe says.

"Time to get a move on things," Tori calls out. "You don't want to be late for your appointment."

"Shall we?" I ask, offering Kendra my hand. She slips hers into mine and I can't stop from lifting it to my lips and pressing a quick kiss there.

"Yes," she says, her voice cracking on the word.

I lead the way, escorting my bride, fake or not; I'm making the most out of this morning.

"I'm surprised Ryker and Aiden aren't here yet," I say to the ladies in the elevator.

"They're just meeting us across the street. I didn't want the room to be too crowded with everyone," Tori says.

We quickly make our way down the elevator and into the lobby. There are a good amount of people milling around as it is now past the normal start of the business day. We walk quickly, hoping that not a lot of people recognize me, but I'm not so sure we're that lucky as I see a few people holding up their cell phones and snapping pictures. *Shit.* We were doing our best to keep this as private as possible. We told very few people and I know the ones that Avery and Tori hired for today are all industry professionals that would keep our identities private unless we gave them the approval to do otherwise.

"Ready?" I whisper for only Kendra to hear as we enter the large building the clerk's office is housed in.

"As I can be," she says, but I can tell she's a little nervous.

"We can always back out if you're having second thoughts."

"No, we've had the opportunity to do that, we're doing this," she states matter of factly. I love seeing the determination in her stance. She's finding that backbone I know she has.

"All right, let's do this, then." I smile and kiss her temple.

The appointment to get our license is smooth. Verify the information we filled out on the online application, agree that we're there on our own accord, and not because someone is forcing us or some shit like that. A few signatures later and we've got a license in our hands.

We take that license over to the next office and wait for our ceremony time. Aiden and Ryker are waiting for the two of us when we arrive with their wives.

"Looking good, man," Ryker says as he slaps my hand and pulls me into a man-hug. "And you look gorgeous," he tells Kendra as he gives her a hug, as well.

"Thank you, they went a little overboard," she says, motioning to Avery and Tori.

"It isn't like you get married every day," Aiden chimes in.

We all chit-chat while Chloe snaps some candid pictures as we wait until our names are called and we can enter to room.

The magistrate explains how they do things, verifies we are who we say we are, as well as checks our license.

"If you are ready, we can get started," she says.

Since this isn't a church, the service is quick, just us

both repeating the basic vows before the magistrate announces us as an officially married couple.

"You may now kiss your bride," she says, smiling at both of us.

I close the space between us, and cup Kendra's cheeks before I bring my lips to hers. The moment we connect, the entire room disappears around us. I don't notice the whoops and hollers from my friends or the click of Chloe's camera shutter.

I have no idea how long I kiss her, I just know I put everything into that one kiss. The sounds of the room come flooding in as we break apart. I press my forehead against hers, looking down into her eyes as she smiles up at me. "You good?" I whisper.

"Perfect," she agrees.

"Damn," I hear Tori say. I look over and she's fanning herself like whatever she's watching is hot.

Aiden says something to her, but I can't hear what exactly it is, but it makes her smile and nod. I don't know why, but something makes me think whatever he said has to do with Kendra and me.

"I'll get your license signed and filed, please make use of the room for the next twenty minutes and I'll be back with your paperwork," the magistrate says.

Chloe jumps right in after that and has us posing for some more pictures.

We finish up and take our paperwork with us. It is crazy to think that is all that it took to go from single to married.

"Well, now what?" Kendra asks as we exit the room.

"We have the hotel room for a few more hours, I

have some snacks being delivered, so let's all head back there and celebrate!" Tori says.

Kendra slips her hand into mine as we make our way out of the building. My fingers slide against the ring I slipped onto her finger just a little bit ago. I thought about it the other day and stopped at a jewelry store on the way home. I knew she wouldn't want anything extravagant, so I controlled myself and didn't splurge much. The way she gasped in surprise when I pulled it out, along with the simple gold band I picked up for her to give me, when we were asked if we'd be exchanging rings. The metal digs into my skin, and I can't help but rub my thumb across it.

"When did you get the rings?" Kendra asks as we walk across the street back to the hotel.

"The other day," I tell her, but don't elaborate.

"Why?" she asks.

I shrug my shoulders. "Just thought it would help sell the whole thing," I tell her. I don't elaborate that I wanted this to feel as real as it possibly could for her. I know it's supposed to be anything but real, but that still doesn't negate the fact that I want her to forget that little part.

We make it back to the room and Tori wasn't lying. There is an entire spread of food laid out on a table, along with a small cake in the center.

"Oh my gosh!" Kendra cries out. "You didn't have to do all of this." She points to the spread.

"Of course I did. You deserve the whole experience," Tori tells her as they hug.

"So, should I expect you to be late tonight?" Ryker

asks as he stands next to me, a plate of finger foods in his hand.

"Uh, no," I tell him as I give him a questioning look.

He holds up his hands like he's backing down. "I just know what it was like on my wedding day. I didn't want to let my wife out of my sight, let alone out of the bedroom." He smirks.

"It isn't like that," I attempt to say, but don't really believe the words that are coming out of my own mouth.

"Keep telling yourself those lies." He chuckles.

"I won't be late," I state. "I take my job seriously, and this won't change that."

"I know you do, but it's okay to also enjoy your life outside of the rink."

"There's time for that after the season," I tell him.

"If you say so." He shrugs. "Doesn't mean that you can't enjoy what life's given you all the time. Embrace it, man, it might just be the best thing to ever happen to you."

I let his words sink in. If there's anyone that knows the trials that life can throw at you, it is Ryker.

We settle in and visit with everyone for a little while. Before we know it, it is time to check out of the room. The girls all help Kendra pack up everything, sending us away with all the leftover food and cake.

Once back at the condo, I manage to get everything upstairs in one trip, thanks to a cart.

"I can get everything put away if you want to go take your nap," Kendra says.

"That isn't necessary," I tell her as I tug her down the hall.

"What are we doing?" she asks, a tremble in her voice.

I stop in my tracks and turn to face her. I slide a lock of hair that has fallen into her face behind her ear, my hand resting on her cheek as I peer down into her eyes. My other hand rests on the side of her bump. I have this irrational want to feel the baby kick, just once. "Can I just hold you? It doesn't have to be anything more than that if you don't want it to be, but I just have this desire to hold you. I can't explain it, but it's soul deep." The words come tumbling out. I've never been so raw and open with a woman, but here I am, opening my heart to this amazing one that is standing in front of me. The one that I just signed and pledged to love and cherish forever.

"Okay." She nods, and it is almost as if I can see the nervousness flee from her body. She places her palm against my hand cupping her cheek. I run the pad of my thumb across her lips, tugging the bottom one down slightly as her tongue slips out, flicking the tip of my thumb. I swear I feel that flick on the tip of my cock and it's instantly hard and pulsing against my zipper. "I never said anything earlier, but you look very handsome in this suit. I don't think I've ever seen you in this one."

I clear my throat. "Thanks, I don't wear it often; it's my most expensive suit. I only pull it out for special occasions."

"This was special for you?" she asks, and I just can't with this woman.

"It isn't every day I marry a beautiful woman." I wink at her.

"Such a charmer." She laughs, and it is the most beautiful sound in the world.

I lead her into my room, straight to the edge of my bed. I slide my hand down her back, over the exposed skin, until I reach the top of her dress. Her eyes meet mine and she must see the question in mine, as no words are exchanged in the moment I slide my hand down her spine, my fingers trailing along ever so slightly until I reach her waist. I tug on her dress, pulling it up and over her belly and then over her head. She does this cute little shimmy shake movement once the garment is off, causing her luscious tits to bounce into my view. My mouth waters as I take in the plump mounds as they sit cupped in her bra.

"May I?" I ask, sliding a hand along the clasp of the garment.

"Yes," she says in a whisper.

I flick the clasp, and the bra falls away instantly, exposing her already hard nipples to my eyes. I bend down, sucking one nipple into my mouth, lavishing it until she's squirming.

"You like that?" I ask, pushing her dress all the way down until it is pooling at our feet.

"Yes, keep going," she practically whines. I chuckle before sucking the other one into my mouth. As my mouth ravishes her breast, my hand lowers until I find the edge of her, apparent, lace underwear. I release her nipple with a pop, then stand to my full height and take in the sight before me.

"Fucking perfect," I growl, seeing the scrap of white lace covering her pussy. "Lie back," I instruct, nodding toward the mattress.

Kendra does as I ask, sitting on the edge before she slides back. She rests her head on one of the pillows, her body on full display for my eyes only. She slides her hand up her body, and I love the way it reacts under my watch. I shuck my suit off, taking a moment to drape it over the chair and not just letting it hit the floor. I strip down to my boxer briefs. I give my cock a quick squeeze as it isn't his turn yet.

I kneel on the mattress, and it dips under my weight as I slide forward and between her legs. I sling one thigh over my shoulder, and she follows suit with the other. I can't help it, I press my face against her center, breathing her in. Her arousal fills my nostrils and my mouth waters.

"Tristan," my name falls from her lips.

"Tell me what you need, beautiful."

"More," she says as she arches her back, pressing her center closer to my face.

"Yes, ma'am." I chuckle and slide what I now realize is a thong to the side. I run my nose up her slit, followed by the tip of my tongue.

"Yes!" She cries out the connection. Her body must be so strung tight to already be arching the way that she is. I part her folds with my fingers, loving how wet and ready she is for me.

I circle her clit with my tongue, waiting until I sink

two fingers inside her pussy to suck it hard between my lips. The moment I do both, Kendra crests over the edge, her orgasm hitting her hard as she arches into my touch. I lick and suck until her body goes limp underneath me. I kiss my way up her body, lapping at her nipples again when I reach them.

I settle in beside her body, letting her relax into my side. When she starts to stir, I take off my boxers and palm my cock. It is still hard and ready to be the star of the show. "Roll away from me," I whisper into Kendra's ear. She does as I ask, and I lift her top leg and rest it on my hip as I fit myself behind her, my cock rubbing her folds from the back. "Ready?" I ask, my voice low and gravely.

"Yes," she says, and I line my cock up with her entrance and push inside. The combination of her body taking me in and the angle has me ready to bust my load and I've only thrust once. I haven't been a minute man since I was a teenager fumbling my way around my first girlfriend's pussy.

I hold on to her, my arm bracing her body as I find her clit with my fingers. "This might be fast and hard," I warn. "I'm already so close."

"I can take it." She peers over her shoulder and the way her desire fills her eyes has my body on fire. I smash my lips to hers, no longer able to hold back. I piston my hips, sliding so easily in and out of her body. My orgasm builds and builds with each snap of our skin. The room is filled with the sounds of our bodies coming together in the most intimate ways possible.

"I can't," I start to warn her as my balls draw up, my

orgasm teetering on the edge. I pinch her clit and feel as her body violently clamps around mine, her orgasm hitting as mine hits me. I slam my cock deep inside her, feeling as I release what has to be the most intense orgasm in my life. I collapse against the bed, kissing her shoulder as I attempt to suck air into my lungs. "That was intense," I say between breaths.

"Best ever," she mumbles in her own blissed out state.

We stay in that position for a few minutes as we both come back down from the high of our orgasms. It's when I pull out that I realize I never put a condom on. No wonder it felt so different. I've never experienced sex without one on.

"Shit," I curse under my breath.

"What's wrong?" Kendra asks as she rolls over to face me.

"I'm so sorry," I say, lowering my head to press against her shoulder.

"What are you sorry about?" she asks, running her fingers through my hair along my scalp.

"I forgot a condom," I say against her skin.

"Oh, well, it isn't like I'll get pregnant," she laughs. "I'm pretty sure I told you before that we could go without," she reminds me.

"You did, I just never have and, well, it wasn't intentional, and for that I'm sorry. Look at me already fucking up this husband thing."

"Oh, stop it." She smacks my shoulder and laughs. "You aren't fucking up anything. Unless it's my lady bits, you can fuck them anytime you want."

I can't hold in the laugh that bubbles up from deep within me. "Is that so?" I ask as I pull her on top of me, my cock already swelling as it sits nestled between her folds.

"Yes," she says as she lifts her hips and slides down my shaft.

The rest of the afternoon follows much the same, until I'm running out of the condo, knowing there's no way I'll get there on time.

Ryker is smirking as I walk into the locker room, a knowing smile tugging at his lips. "Good nap today?" he asks as I tug my dress shirt off.

"The best I've ever had," I quip, not hiding one bit the smile that tugs at my own face.

"Someone finally got laid," Blake, our goalie, calls out from his stall.

"Fuck off," I smart at him as we all get ready to get stretched out and warmed up before it's time to hit the ice.

CHAPTER 20
KENDRA

I take my seat next to Avery, watching as the guys skate circles around the ice and send pucks flying toward the net.

"And how was your afternoon?" She smirks at me.

"Oh, it was good," I tell her and try to hide my blush. "Didn't do much, just got everything put away and napped. Like I said, not much," I try and lie to my friend. All the while, the real memories of this afternoon play on in my mind like my own little porno video.

"Why don't I believe a word of that?" she asks.

"Because she's got that well fucked look all over her face," Tori chimes in. "And if the way Tristan is smiling down on the ice says anything, it doesn't look like much napping occured. Funny how that is just hours after y'all got hitched." Tori eyes me, just daring me to disagree with her.

"Okay, fine, you're right. We couldn't keep our hands off one another. But I did get everything put away, just not until he ran out of the place forty minutes later than he normally leaves."

"Oh, I'm sure the guys didn't let him live that one down." Avery laughs.

"No idea, I haven't heard from him since he left."

We fall into our normal chit-chat while we watch the remainder of warm-ups. The game starts shortly after and is an action-packed game. The starting line kicks things off when Tristan scores on their first attempt only ten seconds into the game.

"Guy gets lucky all afternoon and now is scoring on the ice, as well," Tori teases me. "Maybe he needs game day sex from here on out," she says.

The fun continues as the Shockwaves continue to pummel Detroit. Tristan is having the best game of his career. He manages to score a hat trick before the first period even ends, and by the end of the game, he's scored a fourth goal and assisted on three others. It's no shock to anyone when he's named the first star of the game once it ends.

"Are you sticking around or heading out?" Avery asks as the crowd quickly clears out from the arena.

"I'm waiting for Tristan, tonight," I tell her. "What are the two of you doing?" I ask both Avery and Tori.

"Heading down to wait on our guys," Tori states as she links her arm in mine and Avery's.

We make our way to the elevator that will take us down to the ice level. After our credentials are checked, we're allowed to pass security and be let back into the hallway that leads to the locker room. There are a few other family members here, and we run into the team owner, Nathan, and his wife, Harper. I've met them both once before, but never really spent much time talking to either of them.

"Hi. Kendra, right?" Harper asks.

"Yes," I confirm, "nice to see you again."

"Same. I'm so glad I ran into you tonight. I heard about your meal business and wanted to ask about getting in on ordering," Harper says.

"Oh, thank you," I tell her. I'm shocked and nervous that news of my little gig has made its way to the team's owner.

"I've heard nothing but amazing things about all your meals. Life's been a little crazy and, well, if I can simplify it by not having to cook every night, then sign me up." She laughs and it puts me at ease a little.

"I've only been at this a few weeks and wasn't going to open more spots for a little while longer. If you want to send me an email, I can get back to you when I do, if that's okay?" I tell her.

"Perfect, and dang, girl! Selling out every week is amazing."

"Thanks. I don't want to take on more than I can handle, especially with so much uncertainty around the corner," I say as I rub my bump.

"Understandable. Have you considered hiring someone to help you?"

"Not yet. I'm not quite to the point that I can afford to pay an employee. Tristan helps a little, and Avery and Tori will also stop by sometimes to help me box up orders on pick-up day. Otherwise, I'm getting a good flow down on my prep and cook days."

"Good for you. I look forward to learning more and hopefully trying your meals out soon," Harper says sweetly before she's pulled away by someone who needs something.

"Look at you, rubbing elbows with my boss's wife." Tristan smirks as he stops in front of me.

"You aren't mad, are you?" I ask, nerves taking hold and waiting for the proverbial shoe to drop.

"Why would I be mad? From what I overheard, she wants to become a customer of yours," he says as he cups my face. "And even if she was just talking to you, why would I be mad about that?" he asks, lowering his voice.

"No reason." I quickly look away as I try and blink the tears back. He isn't Chad. He isn't unreasonable and one to fly off the handle at the littlest of things.

"Talk to me," he pleads. My eyes meet his again and I see the sympathy in them.

"Chad didn't like it if I talked to people he thought were important. Even if I didn't start the conversation. He thought I'd say something that would make him look bad," I tell him.

"That's not me. I'd never be mad because you were talking to someone. Hell, you could talk to the president and I'd stand back and just watch you win him over with your kindness."

I nod slightly, letting him know I hear him. It might just take me a little while to get used to no longer being controlled like I was. There's a reason abused women don't always leave their abusers. We're made to believe everything is our fault, and that's hard to un-learn.

3 weeks later

I sit in the waiting room of my doctor's office. I can't believe I'm already twenty weeks pregnant. Half done. I have my ultrasound appointment first, and then will see the doctor for my normal check-up.

"Kendra," a young woman calls my name from the doorway. I get up and head her way.

"Hi, I'm Autumn, I'll be your ultrasound technician today. Are you ready to see this little baby?" she asks as she leads me into the room.

"I am," I tell her.

"Are we finding out the gender?"

"Yes, but can you place it on this card and seal it into the envelope? I'm going to be surprised in a few days."

"Of course! How are you doing it?" she asks as I lie back on the table. I pull down the stretchy panel on my leggings so she can access my belly.

"I'm giving the envelope to one of my friends and she's ordering cupcakes. The center frosting will be either pink or blue."

"How fun! I'll make sure to keep it a secret and include the images of the money shots in an envelope so you have them for after your reveal party."

"Thank you," I tell her as my eyes go to the TV screen. She explains what she's looking at, pointing out my baby's heart, lungs, brain, fingers, and toes. I close my eyes when she's getting the images and putting the information into the envelope. I'm excited to find out with my friends, and especially Tristan. He was so bummed he wouldn't be here today as they're on the road, so this was my compromise so we could still find out together.

"Alright, everything looks great, I can take you to the exam room, now, for your appointment with the doctor."

"Thanks, can I stop in the restroom, first?" I ask. They'd instructed me to make sure I had a full bladder as it helps with getting the images they need.

"Of course, I'll let the nurse know you're doing that, so go ahead and leave your sample on the shelf for them."

"Will do," I tell her as I practically sprint into the bathroom. This baby is already using my bladder as his or her trampoline. I'm not sure how I'm going to make it another twenty weeks and getting larger as the time goes.

"How are you feeling?" Dr. Morgan asks as she comes into the exam room.

"Good, really good, lately," I tell her.

"That's great to hear. Pregnancy has you glowing," she says as she motions for me to lie back. "I looked over the ultrasound images and everything looks perfect with this little one. Measuring exactly where I'd expect and want you to be at."

"That's good."

"Have you had any Braxton hicks contractions or any concerns?" she asks as she measures my stomach.

"Not that I'm aware of, should I be?"

"No, that's a good thing. I'd want to know if you

start to have them this early. The ultrasound didn't show any shortening of your cervix, but that doesn't always indicate that you aren't having them. I just like to ask, at this point. Have you noticed any kicks or movements yet?"

"Maybe. I felt something but wasn't sure if it was the baby kicking or just gas." I chuckle.

"That's also very normal. The first few times it can feel like butterflies or gas, but soon the movements will feel like a true kick or punch from the inside," she says as she helps me sit back up on the table. "How's sex? Comfortable? Any pain?" she asks.

"It's great." I can feel myself blush at her question.

"Good. As your belly gets larger, don't hesitate to try new positions. Some will feel better than others. And sex doesn't just have to be penetration with a penis in the vagina. Having a partner that will explore things with you is important."

"Yeah, we've done some exploring," I admit.

"That's great. Now, don't stop, unless it is uncomfortable or you don't want to, but I promise, you won't hurt the baby and he or she won't remember anything that happens in utero."

"Let me guess, you get asked that by many dads-to-be?"

"At least once a day." She chuckles. "They all think they're going to be the one with the magically long penis that can penetrate the cervix and hit the placenta. I like to tell them, if they're willing to have sex while their significant other is in active, late-stage labor, they can try, but they might end up with their penis chopped off. That usually shuts them up pretty quickly."

I laugh at the visual. "Oh men, hopefully, Tristan isn't one of them."

"You're all good to go, I'll see you back in a month. We still have two more monthly appointments before we switch to twice a month visits. At your next appointment, plan for some extra time as we'll do your one-hour glucose check for gestational diabetes."

"I've heard that the drink is pretty gross." I grimace.

"I'll admit it isn't the best, but it also isn't horrible to chug down. I occasionally have a few patients that just can't get it down, and in those cases, we can switch over to jelly beans, but I like to try the drink option, first."

"Okay," I agree. "I'll see you in a month, then."

I gather my things and head out, stopping at the checkout desk to make my next appointment before I leave for the store. Thanksgiving is next week and, not only is Jackson flying out here for it, but so are my parents and Tristan's parents. Jackson obviously knows about our situation or agreement, but we've somehow managed to keep it a secret from the rest of our families. That will be changing when they all arrive and come over to the condo. I'm a little nervous about dropping the news – sans the part about it being fake.

I head for the store, my list of things I need for this week's meals, along with what I need for when family arrives. I decided to offer a few extra meals this week and take the next off.

"WELL, HOW WAS THE APPOINTMENT?" TORI ASKS WHEN I answer the door. She walks in, Avery on her heels.

"Perfect. Dr. Morgan was happy with everything, said I was right where she wanted me to be."

"So happy for you! Now, where's my envelope?" she greedily asks. I take Carter from her and blow a raspberry in the crook of his neck, which makes him giggle in the best baby way possible.

"Oh, this?" I ask, holding up the envelope for her. She snatches it from my hand and smiles widely.

"Yes!" she exclaims, and she tucks it into her diaper bag.

"No peeking, now," I tease her.

"I can't believe you convinced me to hand it over to the baker without opening it, first. How am I going to buy anything?"

"You'll survive," I laugh at my friend.

"Do you have any feelings one way or the other?" Avery asks.

"Not really. One day I think girl, then, boy the next. I can't make up my mind."

"I think it's a girl," Avery says.

"Same," Tori agrees.

"We'll see!" I tell them. I'm excited to find out in a few days.

"Are your parents excited to find out?" Tori asks.

"I haven't told them we're doing a gender reveal when they're here," I admit. "I've kept most things pretty quiet. I'm still not all that sure they're happy about me being pregnant."

"Honey, don't let their judgment dull your shine," she says, which makes me cry.

"Oh, sweetie, don't cry, I didn't mean to upset you." Tori pulls me into a hug. "It's their loss if they don't want to be involved. Look at how far you've come in just the short time you've been here. I can't think of one other person that has gone through the hell that you have and come out the other side with such an amazing outlook on life. Most people would be jaded as fuck, and rightly so, but what I see in you is truly inspiring."

Avery claps her hands twice, getting our attention. "Okay, enough tears, it's time to celebrate and be happy!" she says in only the way Avery can, with her bubbly personality.

"I meant to ask, how is Ellie? I've missed seeing her at the games the past few weeks."

"She's good. She had a good time visiting her mom for her wedding. Her bridesmaid dress was so gorgeous. She said her stepdad is pretty cool, as well, and she gets along well with his kids, so that's a plus. Once she got back from that, she's just been busy with school, and she's got a boyfriend, now. He's so sweet. Was a little tongue-tied the first time he met Ryker, but he held his own and Ryker is coming around to the idea that his baby is growing up and old enough to be dating. I might have had to hold him back and promise him a BJ one night when they were cuddled up on the couch. He wasn't a fan of how close they were sitting." Avery laughs as she updates us.

"Oh man, I'm sure that was a sight to see. I can

totally imagine Ryker as a bad-ass papa bear when it comes to Ellie," Tori says.

"Yeah." Avery sighs. "He's definitely got that down in spades." I swear I can see little hearts forming in her eyes as she thinks about her husband. "I can't wait to see how he is." She abruptly stops talking and turns beet red.

"*Oh my God!* Are you pregnant?" Tori screams in excitement.

"Well shit, I guess I can't keep a secret." Avery nods, letting us know that she is knocked-up.

"I knew it!" Tori says as she pulls her best friend into a hug. They jump around in excitement together before pulling me into their embrace. I still have Carter in my arms, and he lets his little baby laugh fill the air as he feeds off of our excitement.

"I guess we'll just have babies all around," I say once we've all calmed down.

"Heck yes we will. Think of all the cute baby outfits we can plan for next season. I can already see it now. We'll have the best dressed kids cheering on their daddies," Tori says, and I can help but wince at the term daddy. Tristan might be willing to help me out, but I can't imagine he'll want to be thought of as my baby's father figure.

CHAPTER 21
TRISTAN

THE BUZZER SOUNDS, ALERTING US THAT OUR FAMILY HAS arrived, so I hit the button to let them up. I know Kendra has been nervous for today for the past week, but that anxiety has been through the roof since she woke up this morning. The two orgasms I gave her earlier did little to calm her down for more than an hour.

"Just breathe. It isn't good for either of you for you to get so worked up," I remind her as I slide an arm around her, resting my hand on her belly. She melts into my side, resting her hand on my chest.

"I know, I'm just nervous," she says as there's a knock at the door.

"I'm here for whatever you need," I say as I drop a chaste kiss on her lips before I step out of our embrace and open the door.

Jackson is front and center, pulling me into a huge hug. I slap his back and realize just how much I've missed seeing my best friend. He releases me and steps to the side, taking in Kendra. The way he engulfs her in a hug has me almost choking up and ready to hand over my man card. Instead, I pull my mom into a hug. When she releases me from her grip, I give my dad a man-hug and repeat the same with Jackson and Kendra's parents, as well.

Once we've all exchanged pleasantries, I give them a quick tour of my condo and we get comfortable in the living room, where everyone can find a place to sit.

"How are you feeling these days?" my mom asks Kendra.

"Pretty good. I had my twenty-week checkup last week and everything was perfect, according to my doctor."

"That's great to hear, did you have your ultrasound?" her mom asks.

She doesn't hesitate, a smile pulling up her lips. "I did," she tells her as she stands to grab the packet of pictures they gave her. "Would you like to see?" she asks, and I can hear the hope in her question.

"Of course, I can't wait to see my grandbaby," Denise tells her, and a weight instantly lifts off Kendra's shoulders. I know her mom's words have immediately affected her by the way she sits next to her, showing her all the pictures that we've both looked at numerous times.

"Did you find out the gender?" my mom asks as the pictures are passed around.

"Kind of," Kendra says, biting her lip as she hesitates. Her eyes find mine and I give her a little nod of encouragement. "The technician wrote it down on a piece of paper but put it in a sealed envelope. I then gave that to one of my friends who has ordered cupcakes. They're bringing them over later tonight for all of us to find out together," she tells everyone.

"Oh, how fun!" my mom exclaims. "Sounds like we'll get to go baby shopping while we're here, Denise," my mom says to Kendra's mom.

"Sounds like it," Denise agrees. "And you're good with baby things filling your bachelor pad?" she turns to ask me.

"I am. It's not much of a bachelor pad anymore." I shrug. "I like to think of this place as our home, one I now share with Kendra and, in a few months, the baby," I tell them honestly.

"How did I never see this as our future," my mom muses. "I know we've been friends for a long time, Denise, but something tells me we might be future in-laws."

I watch as all our parents' eyes are on the two of us, and notice the exact moment my mom's eyes notice the ring on Kendra's finger. "What is that?" she jumps up and asks. Kendra tries to pull her hand back, hiding the ring that I put there just a few weeks ago.

"We got married," I blurt out, deciding to rip the Band-Aid off.

"You what?" My dad, of all people, calls out over all the chatter coming from the parents. I look over at Jackson, who is just sitting back and smirking at the shit-show this has turned into. "Did you know?" my dad asks him.

"Yeah, I knew," Jackson confirms as he sits there.

"Okay, spill," my mom says.

"A few weeks ago, we decided to go down to the courthouse and get married. A quick stop at the clerk's office granted us a license and, an hour later, we were walking out a married couple," I quickly recap for them. They don't need the dirty details about *why* we decided to do this on a whim.

"Would you like to see the pictures?" Kendra asks as she stands up. We got a package the other day, and in it was an album, along with a flash drive with all the photos and a release to have them printed if we so desired.

"Of course," my mom says. "I can't believe I wasn't invited to my only son's wedding."

"I knew about it and wasn't even invited," Jackson pipes up. I glare at him, as he isn't really helping, at the moment, but that jackass just smirks at me, knowing that I've made my own pile of shit and now I've got to deal with it.

"Oh my, you were gorgeous," Denise says as she looks at the pictures. "And Tristan, you clean up so nicely," she compliments me when she sees me in my suit.

"It was a beautiful morning," Kendra tells everyone. "Everyone involved made sure it was a special time. We really have our friends to thank, as they did most of it," she says. Her eyes find mine as our parents crowd around, looking through the album. I wink at her, letting her know I haven't forgotten one memory from that day. Especially the one from the few hours after we got back here to the condo.

"So, what does this mean, are you going to adopt the baby?" Mom asks.

"We haven't really figured all that out yet," Kendra answers for me. "I have my first meeting with an attorney next week, to figure out what my options are and how hard it will be to get Chad to sign away his rights to the baby. If he doesn't, and wants to string things along, it will just make it harder and longer for me to fully move on. But knowing him, I don't really expect him to make anything easy. I'm hoping my attorney can make the idea of not being on the hook for child support if he signs his rights away be too good of a trade-off to not do it."

"And if he isn't cooperative?" my dad asks.

"Then, we'll do whatever it takes, no matter how long it takes," I tell him, my assertiveness hopefully coming through loud and clear to everyone that I'm here to stay.

"Well, what a day! So many surprises." Mom adds, "Are you making the extra room into a nursery, then?"

Kendra looks at me, as we hadn't discussed this yet, but it only makes sense. She's been sleeping in my bed every night since we got married.

"I think so, unless she wants the baby in our room to start with," I say and smirk to myself as Jackson grunts from where he sits. I'm pretty sure I just heard him mutter a death threat my way. I never told him about our sleeping arrangements and I don't think Kendra has, either, not that it is really any of his business.

"I think both options will work," Kendra confirms. "I've read that it is nice to keep the baby bedside for the first couple of months, especially with nighttime nursing. Then, move them to their own room once sleeping through the night all the time."

"Whatever you want," I tell her.

"Aww, I never thought I'd see the day." My mom moves over next to me. She pats my face before leaning in to kiss my cheek. "My baby boy is growing up into such an amazing young man. I'm so happy you're happy."

"I'm happy, Mom," I assure her. "Never thought I could be this content, but what can I say? I guess it took the right person to change my outlook."

My eyes flick to Kendra, and I see the hope in her dark orbs. I hope she can tell I'm not just feeding our parents a line of BS.

Once the excitement of finding out the gender in just a few hours and the shock about our wedding wears off, the conversation flows. Kendra fills everyone in on how her business is growing and how she has a waiting list of potential new clients. After the holidays, she plans to take on a few more, but slowly, which I keep telling her is a great plan. There is no reason for her to scale up too quickly. I don't want her burning out or taking on too much, especially as her energy wanes as her pregnancy progresses.

"This spread looks amazing, you've outdone yourself," Mom tells Kendra as we all take our seats at the table.

"Thank you. I started prepping yesterday so that I wouldn't be doing it all today. I also have some things prepped for Thanksgiving already, as well."

"Very smart," her mom tells her as we all start to dig in to the pans of lasagna, the huge bowl of salad and plate piled high with homemade garlic bread. I love the days she makes homemade bread. It always smells so damn good in here on those days.

"Oh my god, sis," Jackson says around a full mouth of bread.

"You like?" she asks, perking up.

"No." He shakes his head as he shoves another large bite in. "I love it," he follows up once he can talk again with an empty mouth.

"I've been working on my bread making and have gotten pretty good at it, if I do say so myself."

"If the meals you make and sell are even half as good as this one, I see why you have a waiting list," her dad praises her.

"Thanks, Dad," she replies, a slight blush tinting her cheeks. One thing I've learned since Kendra has lived with me, is she isn't used to being praised, so when she is, she gets embarrassed easily. I've been doing my damnedest to change that, praising her as often as I can. My favorite time is when I'm between her legs with my tongue, making her come undone. My body tenses at the dirty thoughts, a little more obvious than I was expecting.

"Something wrong?" Jackson asks from his seat beside me.

"Nope," I tell him as I shove a large bite into my mouth and will my cock to deflate. The absolute last thing I need is to have a hard-on with our family all around us.

CHAPTER 22
KENDRA

I SIT AT THE TABLE, TAKING IN OUR FAMILY SURROUNDING us; our friends who have become like family in such a short amount of time. Tori sets the platter of cupcakes down in the center of the table for everyone to pick from. They are so delicately decorated, a swirl of pink and blue frosting on top.

"All right, last chance to change your guess to what you think the center icing will be," Tori instructs.

When she arrived, she went around asking everyone their guess, and handed out either pink or blue stickers based on the answer she received. The room is split almost down the middle, with seven people thinking girl and five thinking boy.

No one jumps at her offer to change their guess, so we all pick our cupcake and on the count of three, all bite into them.

Pink frosting coats the inside and the fact that I'm having a girl hits me. A daughter.

"It's a girl!" Tristan's mom, Kristen, calls out, her excitement evident.

I'm pulled into hugs by everyone, Tristan being the last one to finally wrap his arms around me. "Congratulations. Do you have a name in mind yet?" he asks.

"No, not yet," I tell him. I have hesitated even looking at the baby name book that Tori brought over after my appointment. "Maybe we can look together, sometime?" I ask him.

My statement is half question half offer and he chokes up slightly as he thinks it over. "Of course," he says before kissing my temple. I let the affection wash over me. He's definitely upped it since the wedding. It was like that moment flipped a switch and the lines of this being for a fake reason are starting to really blur into nothingness. How I'll get through this heartbreak when everything is over, I don't know. It will be worse than anything I ever lived through with my ex, because when this ends, my heart will shatter because even though I knew the outcome, I'm in love with my husband.

"I THINK WE SHOULD MAKE A LIST OF THE THINGS YOU most need and want, and then go from there," my mom suggests as we start flipping through all the Black Friday ads for tomorrow's sales.

"That's a good idea. I also need to start my registry, but that isn't something for tomorrow." I laugh.

"Definitely not. Maybe you can set it up online? Just

add things from the comfort of home?" Kristen suggests.

"Probably, and I like that idea. I've started researching brands and what items have the best ratings, both from parents and safety testing."

"Gosh, there are a lot of baby things. Not much of this was a thing when you kids were babies," my mom says as she flips through one of the baby ads.

"I can only imagine how things have changed in twenty-something years."

"What would you like to shop for tomorrow?" Kristen asks.

"I really have no idea. Probably not any of the big furniture. I need to make some nursery decisions before that kind of stuff can be picked out."

"That's understandable. What about the stroller and car seat, it looks like a lot of sets are on sale."

"That would be a good thing to check for," I agree, adding it to my list.

"There are also deals on all the basics, like baby bath items, diapers, bottles, just about the entire section will be on sale," Mom says.

"Sounds like a trip through the baby aisles is where we need to start, then," Kristen jokes with my mom. "Watch out world, the grandmas will be on the loose and are ready to shop," Kristen adds.

I can't help but smile at our moms' antics. They are both so excited and that is such a weight off of my shoulders. Why I ever thought they wouldn't be, I don't know, but now that they're up to date on everything,

I'm mad at myself for keeping them both at a distance these past few months.

I SLIDE INTO BED; THE COOL SHEETS FEEL GOOD AGAINST MY hot skin. Pregnancy has done a few things to me, and one of them is to turn me into a damn furnace. I swear, I'm always hot and ready to strip down to my birthday suit.

"How are you doing?" Tristan asks as he pulls me closer, his own naked body wrapping around mine. Even with being hot, I don't mind the contact between the two of us.

"Exhausted. I'm not sure how I'm going to make it shopping all day. I think our mothers have every store that might possibly sell baby items on the list of places to stop at tomorrow," I tell him.

"Then, let them go and you can stay here and relax," he suggests.

"Maybe." I cover a yawn that I can't hold back.

"Sleep, beautiful, you need your rest." He kisses the top of my head as I drift off to sleep.

I wake up, needing to pee thanks to this baby girl using my bladder as a trampoline, apparently. Tristan is curled up behind me, spooning his body around mine. I've come to love sleeping in his arms, they are quite comforting. His arm is slung around me, his hand resting on my bump, so I lift it up so I can slide out of bed and get to the bathroom.

"Where are you going?" he mumbles in his sleepy state.

"Just to the bathroom, I'll be back in a minute," I assure him.

There isn't much light peeking in the windows, so I'm hopeful that I can go back to sleep after my bathroom break. I quickly do my business, then stop to wash my hands before heading back to bed. I take in Tristan's sleeping form. He's rolled onto his back, the sheet has slipped down, and is now riding low on his hips. His abs look like chiseled stone beneath the ink that covers his beautiful body.

"How long are you going to just stare at me?" he asks.

I didn't even realize his eyes were open. I thought he was sound asleep.

"Sorry," I say as I reach for the glass of water I keep next to the bed. I drain the little bit that is left, then turn and head to the kitchen to refill it. I return, setting the cup back on the nightstand and then slipping back into bed.

"That's better," Tristan mumbles as I curl up with him. I drape my leg over his and rest my hand on his chest, pressing my front to his side as I get comfortable. I can't miss the thickness of his cock near my leg. He likes to sleep naked, so waking up to him pressed against me, hard, isn't unusual.

"Someone is awake this morning," I tease as his dick twitches.

"I can't help it when my wife is naked and curled up next to me," he says, and rolls over so he's hovering over me. "Mornin', beautiful," he huskily says as his lips find mine.

He settles his hips between my legs; his hard cock slips through my folds, hitting my clit with each lazy thrust and rotation he makes. My body is wet and ready for him as I kiss him deeply.

There are no words needed. Tristan reaches down and aligns his cock with my entrance. His tip easily slides in before he makes one thrust and is fully filling me.

"Yes," I cry out as I break from the kiss. My body arches into his, ready to take him as deep as I can in this position, which doesn't feel that deep with my belly starting to get in the way.

Tristan thrusts a few times before pushing back on his haunches and pulling out. "Roll over," he instructs, and I do as asked. He slides off the bed and I follow him to the edge. He lines himself back up with my opening and slides in deep, this time all the way, practically hitting my cervix with his tip. "You good?" he asks.

"Yes, fuck me hard," I tell him as I roll my head to the side as I rest my cheek on the mattress.

"Your wish is my command," he says as he grips my hips and starts a punishing rhythm. It doesn't take long for my climax to build, but just when I think I'm going to crest over the edge, he slows down, leaning his large body over mine, his front covering my back as his lips find the shell of my ear. "Not yet, I want you crying my name when you come hard on this dick."

I can't help but whimper. I know that he'll build me

back up and let me come soon, all in the name of my pleasure.

"Please," I plead. I reach my hand down and start rubbing at my clit.

"No," he barks, moving my hand away as he slides out and flips me over on the bed, tugging me until my ass is at the edge once again. "I'll make you come," he says as he lowers his body down, kneeling at the edge of the bed. He licks up my center, and my body quakes from his touch. The combination of his warm breath on my wet skin and the sensation his tongue brings to the mix has my body on fire and ready to combust.

Tristan sucks my clit between his lips, flicking the nub with his tongue as he slips two fingers inside me. The moment he finds my g-spot, I crest and combust in the most excellent of ways. I see stars as my body goes rigid; my thighs squeeze around his head, holding him tightly against my center as he laps at my release.

"Good girl," he purrs as he stands back up, wiping at his lips with the back of his hand. He rubs his cock through my folds again, coating it with more of my release. Once my body is relaxed and like jello, he slips inside of me, back to lazy thrusts as he holds himself off of my belly but still manages to lean forward and kiss me soundly. "That's it, baby, come again for me. Coat this cock with your cum." His dirty words do the trick as he slides in and out. He presses a thumb to my clit with one hand, and tweaks one of my nipples with the other. I can't stop the orgasm from happening, not that I'd really want to. I just enjoy the ride as he increases his pace, thrusting through my tightness as he finds his own pleasure.

Tristan's forehead lands on my shoulder as he sucks in large gulps of air. Our bodies both languid and in that immediate bliss that only mutual orgasms can create.

"Good morning," I say, my voice all sex-drunk.

"Indeed it is." He chuckles and pulls out, reaching for a washcloth from the nightstand where we've started keeping them for easy cleanup. "What time are you going shopping today?" he asks.

"I think around nine. I told our moms last night that I wasn't interested in being out at four or five this morning when the stores opened with large crowds. I knew I wouldn't last long getting up that early."

"I don't blame you. How about some breakfast before you go?" he offers.

"I'd like that. I'm going to go grab a quick shower, first."

"While you shower, I'll go whip something up, any requests?" he asks as he helps me stand. I love the way he holds me close to his body, resting a hand on my belly as he does.

"Mhmm," I hum, thinking of what sounds good right now. "Maybe some strawberry crepes. I think we still have some made up in the fridge. I know there is the vanilla filling, so all you'd have to do is heat them up, add the filling and some cut strawberries."

"Sounds easy enough. Do you want any eggs or bacon on the side? Maybe some sausage?" He winks, and I don't miss the sexual innuendo.

"I've already had my fill of sausage this morning," I grin, bumping my hip into him.

"You can never have too much of this," he teases right back, pressing his half-hard cock against me.

"You're incorrigible." I laugh and push him away. "I'm going to shower, now, you go make me some food. This baby momma is hungry." I point toward the bedroom door, instructing him where I want him to go. He just laughs at me before walking over to the dresser and grabbing a clean pair of boxer briefs from the top, then sliding on a pair of athletic shorts he pulled out from another drawer. He doesn't bother putting a shirt on, and I can't say I mind one bit at all. As he leaves the bedroom, I get to moving so I can take that shower I've been saying I was going to take for the last fifteen minutes.

I'm fresh and clean, even decided to put a little makeup on while I was getting ready. I feel so good this morning. I'm not sure if that is because of how amazing it was last night with our family, the intense orgasms from this morning, or the shopping trip in a little bit that has me feeling like I'm on top of the world, right now. I just worry slightly that this feeling is going to come crashing down and I won't be able to stop it.

"Well, don't you just look glowing," my mom says as I enter the living room.

"Thank you. Have you been here long?" I ask, accepting the hug she offers.

"Maybe five minutes," she says, looking at her watch.

"Oh good, have you eaten breakfast yet? Tristan was going to warm us up something."

"I grabbed a muffin at the hotel, figured I'd get something else along the way this morning."

"You're welcome to eat here before we go," I offer.

"If it is whatever that lovely smell is coming from the kitchen, then yes, please," Mom says as we both head to the kitchen. Tristan's mom, Kristen, is next to him, helping him plate up the crepes, adding a final dash of powdered sugar to the top before she slides the plates across the island.

"This looks amazing," I tell them as I approach.

"I wouldn't expect anything less, now that I know how good of a cook you are," Kristen praises me.

"Hey now, I should get some credit. I heated them up today," Tristan pretend pouts, sticking out his bottom lip as he tries to sell it.

"Of course you do." Kristen pats Tristan's chest as she plays into his antics.

Breakfast is amazing, and after we're done, the three of us head out to go check out the Black Friday sales. I try and resist tossing things into the cart while we're walking through the baby aisles, but my mom and Kristen both have no self-control, tossing so many things into the cart.

After what feels like an entire week, but realizing is only a portion of the day, we finally return back home and unload everything that was purchased today. We sort through everything, piling up the diapers in one corner of the spare bedroom that will soon be turned into the nursery. Sorted all the cute baby outfits by size and I left them in piles for when it is time to actually put them away in a dresser that I need to purchase, at some point.

———

THE PAST FEW DAYS WITH OUR PARENTS HERE FLEW BY before I knew it. I'm so glad they all came out to visit, as it was great to spend time with everyone, especially since I had such amazing news to share with them.

I've been feeling a little uneasy since last night, as my appointment with the attorney Avery recommended I meet with is today. She's a busy woman, and this was the first opening she had.

After everyone left yesterday, I was so jittery, Tristan picked me up, carried me into the bathroom, made me take a relaxing bath, then fucked me slowly until I was so tired I couldn't keep my eyes open. It's amazing how good sex can be such a good distraction when my mind is racing a million miles an hour.

"Hi, how can I help you?" the older woman behind a desk asks as I step into the law office.

"Hello, I'm Kendra Torres, I have a ten thirty with Lucy Montgomery," I tell the older lady.

"Of course, dear, she's just finishing up on a call. Can I get you anything while you wait? Coffee, water, tea?" she asks.

"I'm good, but thanks," I tell her before taking a seat on one of the chairs in the large waiting room.

I take in my surroundings and realize this place is filled with expensive things. I start to panic inside, not knowing how exactly I'm going to be able to afford this lawyer's help.

"Ms. Torres, Ms. Montgomery is available now and is ready for you to come back, if you'd please follow me."

I follow the receptionist down the hall and through a doorway with Ms. Lucy Montgomery, Attorney at Law scrolled across a name plate.

"Hello, so nice to meet you in person, please have a seat," Ms. Montgomery says as she motions to the large, comfy seats that are across the desk from her.

"Thank you," I say, both to her and the older woman who showed me into her office. "It's nice to meet you, Ms. Montgomery, as well. Avery speaks highly of you."

"She's great, isn't she? And please, call me Lucy. How are you holding up?"

"Okay, I think." I give her a small smile, hoping that my nerves aren't giving me away.

"So I take it your nerves are making it so you can barely function?" She smiles wide at me.

"Basically," I confirm.

"Well, take a few breaths, I think you're going to like what I have to tell you," she says and opens a file folder on her desk. She pulls out a few pieces of paper, looking over them before turning her attention back to me. "I've pulled all the court records and done a deep dive into Mr. Barlow's charges. I don't think he'll be seeing the outside of a jail cell much for many, many years. Because of that, I think we've got a good shot at him signing away his rights from the get-go," she goes on to explain.

"Can I ask why you're so confident that it will be easy?" I ask her.

She gives me a devilish grin. "I'm not sure how much Avery told you about me, but I'm a bulldog when it comes to fighting for my clients. I read the doctors' reports from your time in the hospital. A judge isn't going to like hearing all those details, much less a jury. After talking with the DA on the case, it sounds like they are about to offer a plea bargain to him. My approach is to submit our request to him to terminate all rights before the baby is even born. This will free you up from having to place his name on the birth certificate and will also alleviate him from being responsible for any child support, and or expenses for the child."

"And you think he'll agree to the request without a fight?" I ask.

"I do. I'll put it in very plain and simple terms for him. Laying it all out that if he fights us on this, not only will a judge rule in our favor, that judge will also make him responsible for any and all of your attorney fees, court fees and any child support that occurs, up to that point. It could be processed quickly, or the courts could drag on and the amount he'd end up owing will grow into the tens of thousands."

"Okay, so what do you need from me?" I ask.

"I just need you to sign a few papers and then I'll do the rest. My paralegal or myself will be in contact with you as things progress, keeping you informed as to the status of where things are, but it's my hope to have this all wrapped up for you in just a few weeks, at most."

I swallow hard, not quite believing this could all be over so soon. "Okay, tell me where to sign." I smile at her nervously. "Actually, before I do, I need to ask one more question."

Her kind smile helps settle my nerves, although, I'm still nervous how much this is going to cost. Just another thing I'll have to find some way to pay Tristan back for once I'm completely on my own two feet. "What's that?" she asks.

"What do your services cost? I have a very tiny bit of savings, but I'm mostly relying on some friends and family right now. Tristan has offered to cover your costs, but I plan to pay him back when I can," I explain to her.

Her smile widens as she takes in my word vomit. "You can let that worry and weight of how you're going to pay for this rest. I'm providing my services pro-bono," she tells me.

My jaw drops when I realize what that means. "I-I, don't even know what to say." I stumble over my words. "Thank you, but why?" I ask.

"We believe in giving back in this firm. Each attorney is required to have so many pro-bono hours every year. I like to use mine for situations like yours. Single moms have a special place in my heart as I was raised by one. I saw everything she went through to fight for my siblings and me. I noticed the many nights she went without dinner because there just wasn't enough food for all of us, or the days she had to stop and bring home whatever food she could from the local church food closet or food pantry. Paying for an attorney to go after my dead-beat dad for child support wasn't something she could have ever paid for, so if I can make a few women's lives easier by providing my services for free, then I'll do it."

"Thank you, I appreciate it. I'm not sure I feel worthy of the gift, but I also know not to turn down an offer like this."

"Even if you'd said no, I wouldn't have changed my mind."

I nod in acceptance of her words and offer. We go over the documents she'd already prepared before I arrived, and I sign everywhere she needs me to sign before Lucy walks me out of her office and back to the waiting room, where we bid each other goodbye.

I can't believe the outcome of my meeting; I drive home in a daze. I just hope that it goes as quickly and smoothly as she is predicting that it will.

CHAPTER 23
TRISTAN

6 Months later

I STAND IN THE DOORWAY OF MY OLD SPARE ROOM, watching my girls as they slowly rock back and forth in the glider. The room that I finally convinced Kendra into making the nursery. She was very hesitant to do so, said that we should keep it as a spare for when she moved out. The thought of that happening kills me. Watching her with her daughter is one of my favorite things to watch when I'm at home. She's a natural when it comes to being a mother.

She welcomed sweet baby Olivia Marie into the world a month ago and that baby girl has me wrapped tightly around her baby finger.

"How long are you going to stand there staring at us?" Kendra asks as she looks down at the baby as she nurses.

"Didn't want to interrupt your bonding time," I say quietly as I enter the room, coming to sit on the foot stool in front of her. I lean forward and slide my fingers along Olivia's head before rubbing at the back of her closed fist. She opens it and I slip a finger into her grasp. She immediately claps onto my digit, holding it tightly.

Having a newborn in the house has been an adjustment. I didn't realize that such a little thing could make so much noise, messes, and don't even get me started on the smells this little girl can produce. She's a pooping machine, some days.

"We should be done soon," Kendra tells me. I can see the exhaustion in her eyes as they find mine. "She's been eating for awhile now."

"No rush, but once she is done, why don't you let me take over baby duty while you go get a shower and maybe a nap in?" I ask encouragingly.

"A nap sounds like pure heaven. She's cluster feeding again, so must be ready for a growth spurt."

"I'm sorry. At least I'll be here for the next week and can help out," I remind her. It has sucked to leave for road games this past month. I took two personal days when Olivia was born, nothing major, those days, just missed practices. She really did pick the perfect time to give birth while I was in town and just a few blocks away.

"You don't have to," she starts to object like she's done for the last month.

"I know I don't have to, but I want to."

"Okay," she gives in quickly, the exhaustion making it hard for her to argue with me.

Olivia releases Kendra's nipple, a few drops of milk

dribbling out of her mouth. She's got that perfect milk drunk look about her and I can't help but smile at the way she looks so happy.

"Let me take her and you go have some alone time."

Kendra secures her nursing bra, tucking everything back into her shirt. She was somewhat shy about the amount of time her body was exposed right after Olivia was born, even after all the times I saw her completely naked while she was pregnant. I don't care what state her body is in, I still find her sexy. Once she's completely covered, she dabs at the corners of Olivia's mouth, wiping away the remnants of milk that was lingering.

"She should be good for a few hours," Kendra says as she transfers Olivia to my arms. I tuck the baby to my chest, loving how easily she snuggles right into the center. "As least, that's what I'm hoping for."

"I've got her, go take care of yourself. I'll come get you when we need you." I shoo her out of the room before I gather a few necessities—burp rag, small blanket, and one diaper, and a small package of wipes, before heading for the living room. I get settled on the couch, Olivia still sleeping on my chest. I rub her back lightly as I gently kiss the top of her bald head. I get the idea to snap a couple of pictures of the two of us relaxing together and shoot them off to Jackson, and then to my mom.

JACKSON

It's weird to see you with a baby, even if she is the cutest thing on this earth.

MOM

Oh my! Look at how cute the two of you are! She's grown so much in just a few weeks. We really need to get a trip booked out there to meet her in person.

I agree man, she is damn cute. Especially when she pouts and sticks her bottom lip out and lets out a wail of a cry. When are you making it out this way?

You know you're welcome to visit whenever you want. Just say the word and I'll book you a flight and hotel.

JACKSON

I really need to figure that out. Maybe Gabby and I can come out together.

I take it things are still going well then?

JACKSON

They are. We discussed moving in together once our leases both expire. Conveniently enough, they both expire at the same time, so we're going to start searching for a place in just a few weeks.

Happy for you, man.

JACKSON

Thanks man. I'll talk to Gabs about us coming out. I know she'd like to get out there to see both of you and meet the baby, it's just a matter of her actually taking some time off. She hates leaving her patients with the potential of having to see another doctor.

Well keep me posted.

MOM

I'll check my calendar and see when Dad and I can make it out. Maybe we'll get lucky, and you'll have some home games.

Better make it quick, we're in the thick of playoffs.

MOM

I'm aware. How's Kendra doing?

Exhausted most of the time. I took Olivia from her just before sending you the picture and told her to go take a shower and a nap. She said Olivia is cluster feeding, whatever that means. Sounds like she's been keeping her up a lot lately.

MOM

Ah yes, cluster feeds. It's exhausting. Good for you for stepping in and making her take some time for herself. It's important for new moms to have that support.

I do my best, hate it when I have to leave for days at a time. I'm just thankful that Tori and Avery have been helping out when I'm gone. I think they've both caught on to the fact that Kendra won't ask for help, but when you insist, she gladly takes it.

MOM

Good friends are priceless. I'm glad she's found some good ones.

Me too mom, me too.

I set my phone down on the end table and get comfortable. My eyes are heavy as I listen to an old movie on the TV, and before I know it, I'm drifting off to sleep. I wake up the moment I hear her cry, the wail of a pissed-off baby.

"Shh, shh." I pat Olivia's back as I try and calm her down. I pat around for her pacifier, finally finding one on the coffee table. I rub it along her bottom lip, just the way Kendra has shown me. Olivia latches on, sucking vigorously between wails. I think she might be hungry again with the way she isn't satisfied with the pacifier. "Let's get you changed, baby girl. Then, we can go in search of Mommy for some food," I croon to the baby.

She's finally opened her little eyes; they move to take me in as I talk to her as I'm laying her down on the couch. I slip the blanket underneath her body, not wanting any surprises landing on my couch, if I can help it. We've had some unpleasant diaper changes in the last few weeks. I can't help but grimace at the smell that is coming from this little peanut. Once on her back, she pulls her little legs up, letting one rip as she does.

"Did that feel good?" I ask Olivia as I rub her belly, then move her legs like she's riding a bicycle. Kendra showed me that trick after the pediatrician told her to try it when Olivia was grunting and crying every evening. Apparently, it can help babies pass gas or poop if they're having issues. "Now, let's get you all cleaned up and go find Mommy," I coo at her again as I make quick work of changing her diaper. I'd never have thought I'd change diapers, best yet, become a pro at it, but here I am, doing just that. If the guys could see me now. I chuckle as I realize some of them have seen me with Olivia.

I get Olivia zipped back into her sleeper, take the biohazard of a diaper to the trash can, then head for the bedroom to wake Kendra up so she can feed Olivia. I open the door as quietly as I can, using the small amount of light that peeks in from the curtains to make my way over to the bed where Kendra is sleeping soundly. I gently rub her shoulder, wanting to wake he as gently as I can. She bolts upright, seconds after Olivia lets out a cry.

"What's wrong?" she asks groggily.

"Nothing's wrong, someone has a clean butt and an empty stomach," I tell her as I move Olivia around in my arms, prepping to hand her over to her mother. I kiss her cheeks as Kendra adjusts how she's lying on the bed, moving so she can nurse her while she lies on her side. Once she's ready, I place Olivia next to her and take a seat on my side of the bed, lying down so I'm facing them.

Olivia doesn't hesitate to latch on, greedily sucking the milk down.

"Slow down, baby girl, you're going to choke yourself," I tell her as I rub her cheek. She doesn't listen, just continues to eat like she didn't just do this a couple of hours ago. I turn my attention to Kendra. Her eyes are still sleepy, but much better than they were before. "How was your shower and nap?" I ask.

"The best few hours I could have asked for, thank you." She smiles at me over Olivia's body.

"Once she's done eating, I can take her again. We had some great snuggling time."

"You can't hold her all the time while she sleeps," Kendra insists.

"Say's who?" I ask, not liking the thought of that.

"Me, the doctors, all the baby books," she says a little expressively. "If you do it too much, then she'll learn to only sleep if being held. I can't hold her twenty-four-seven and still get anything done. So, once she falls asleep, she really needs to be put in her crib or bassinet."

I push out my bottom lip, sad that I can't just hold her all the time. "But I love having her asleep on my chest. It's very soothing," I try and plead my case.

"I understand, I really do, but please do this for me. You aren't always here for me to take a nap or shower."

"You know you can call Avery or Tori anytime you need help, and they'd drop everything to help you."

"I know, I just hate bothering people."

"Asking for help isn't bothering people."

She just gives me a look like she agrees, but doesn't want to admit that, so silence it is. I lie there and just watch the two of them, soaking in all these moments while Olivia is small. My mom wasn't lying, she has changed so much in the weeks since she was born.

"It's getting close to dinnertime. I can heat something up or order something in, what's your preference?" I ask Kendra.

"I don't really care. We have a few freezer meals ready to go, all you've got to do is pop them in the oven for whatever the top instructions say."

"Easy enough," I tell her. I lean over and kiss the top of Olivia's head before pressing my lips to Kendra's. She's pulled away from me some since Olivia was born, and I get that. She's recovering from nine months of being pregnant, healing from a vaginal delivery, healing from her past relationship that gave her this beautiful little girl that has us both wrapped around her little fingers. She actually kisses me back, which causes my dick to twitch. *Not now, big man,* I think to myself as I imagine what the locker room smells like after a full practice or game. My cock immediately deflates, which is what I was hoping to do.

I head for the kitchen. I rummage through the freezer, checking what options we have. I find a chicken pot pie that just needs to be baked. As soon as I read the labels on each meal, I knew this one was it. I preheat the oven, checking my phone while I wait for it to heat up, then slide it in and set the timer on my phone for when it should be done.

"Thank you for all this," Kendra says as she takes a bite of the food.

"I didn't do much, just baked it and dumped some washed lettuce into a bowl." I try and brush off her compliment.

"I got a call before you got home today," Kendra says after we've both eaten at least half of our food.

"From who?" I ask.

"Lucy," she says, and a smile breaks out on her face. "It's all done, the judge signed off on all the paperwork."

"That's amazing," I tell her as I stand and pull her out of her own seat and into my arms. The dread hits me while she's in my arms. Now that Chad is completely out of the picture, will she need me anymore? Will she *want* me anymore? "So, what's next?" I ask through the turmoil going on in my mind.

"I-I'm not sure. I guess nothing, for now. We continue as we have been until we get to the agreed upon date. I probably need to start searching for a commercial kitchen to rent, especially if I'm going to expand like I'd planned after I go back from my maternity leave."

"You know there's no rush for you to move out of here, right?" I ask, hoping she can see my desperation to keep them both here, where I feel they belong.

"I know, but I'm sure you're ready to get back to your normal life," she starts to say.

"I'm right where I want to be, with whom I want to be with," I tell her firmly. She nibbles on her bottom lip, her eyes searching mine as she does. I take her hands in mine, linking our fingers like that will keep her mine forever. I've pussyfooted around this for months now, but I guess it's time that I man up and lay it all out on the table. "Kendra," I say, my voice cracking, so I clear my throat before I continue on. "What started out as a way to help you get back on your feet, turned into so much more. I never thought I'd be the type of man to settle down and want a family, but now that I've experienced it with the two of you, I can't think of anything better. Having you in my life, in my bed, being married to you, has changed me in here," I tell her as I tap our clasped hands over my heart. "I've always loved you as Jackson's little sister, but that all changed when I fell in love with you as the amazing woman you are." She gasps at my revelation, her eyes are shiny with tears, and I wipe at the few that fall down her cheeks.

"What are you saying?" she asks.

"I'm saying that I don't want you and Olivia to go anywhere. I love both of you so fucking much it hurts. I want to build this life with you that we've started. I want to give that little girl everything she could possibly dream of, and one day, if you agree with it, my last name. I've already given you the opportunity to take it, she might as well have a matching one."

"You love me?" she asks, teary-eyed.

"So, fucking much," I reiterate, pulling her even closer to my body.

"I love you, too," she says, her smile full as she looks up at me.

"Those are the four sweetest words I've ever heard," I tell her before kissing her deeply. My cock swells between us, but I do my best to ignore him, as he's not getting any kind of attention unless it comes from my hand for at least a few more weeks.

We kiss and hold one another for what feels like hours. I'm pretty sure it is only minutes, seeing as how Olivia only sleeps for a max of three hours at a time, and we already spent some of it eating.

"Does this mean that you're staying?" I ask, nervous that she's still going to move out and away from me.

"Yes," she easily agrees.

"Can we burn the agreement to end our marriage, then?" I ask.

"Are you sure you don't want that easy out?"

"Never. I'm in this one hundred percent. The only time I want one of us moving out of this place is if all three of us are moving out to a bigger house or a new city if, for some reason, I was to get traded. We can decide later where we want to call home once I retire, which will hopefully be in five or more years, but only time will tell on that piece of the puzzle."

"I can't believe we're really doing this." Kendra cries and laughs at the same time.

I pick her up, spinning us in a circle. "Believe it, baby. It's you and me against the world, and I'm ready to take it all on with you by my side."

EPILOGUE

Kendra
On our first anniversary

I HOLD THE ENVELOPE IN MY HAND, THE PAPERWORK ALL filled out and ready for a few signatures. I met with Lucy Montgomery this morning while Tristan was at practice, finalizing the petition for adoption.

We've come a long way in the last six months. After that night, when he poured his heart out to me, telling me that he was in this for real, not just a pretend thing to help me out, we really found our groove as a couple. The months of pretending were great practice, but after that day, we opened up more, not only to one another, but to everyone. We didn't hide our relationship as much from the entire team, and that also meant the press. Olivia and my pictures started popping up on social media pages as being his "girls" and while it was something new to deal with at first, I embraced it and things got better. Tristan came to my defense after one tabloid ran a trash story, trying to claim I was trapping him into our relationship with my child. We made the decision for the press release to include that Olivia wasn't his biological child, thus the tabloids were spreading lies about us. Thankfully, that was the only negative story ran, and for the most part, we're left alone.

I've prepared Tristan's favorite dinner for tonight. I contemplated throwing a big party and surprising him with the papers then, but decided that a little thing with just the three of us was a much better plan. It's also our anniversary, if that's what we're calling today. One year ago, we signed our names on the dotted line, promising to love and cherish one another until death do us part, all while knowing in the backs of our minds that we already had an end date circled on the calendar. Little did we know that fate would play a much bigger part in our story.

"Hey." Tristan's sexy voice filters into my mind. I stir on the bed, rolling my head over to see his smiling face. "Sorry to wake you, how long has she been sleeping?" he asks, nodding his head in Olivia's direction. I apparently dozed off with her as she nursed before naptime.

I slip out of bed, doing my best not to wake her up. We both tiptoe out of the room, closing the door behind us as quietly as we can.

I check the time on my watch. "I think about an hour or so. Hopefully, she stays put for another hour," I tell him.

"Perfect amount of time, then." He smirks and pulls me into his arms.

"For what?" I ask as I go easily.

"For me to make love to my wife," he says before kissing me. "We need to celebrate our anniversary, and since you vetoed going out tonight." Another kiss. "I guess I'll just have you for my afternoon snack." He picks me up and carries me to the couch, since our bed is currently occupied.

Tristan sits down on the couch, pulling me down to straddle his lap. His erection is already hard and ready to burst out of his pants. I grind my center against him, loving the pressure it provides against my already throbbing clit. "You ready to scream my name?" Tristan growls as he nips at my jaw.

"Yes," I pant as he lifts me up and tugs my leggings down. I reach down and pull at the elastic waistband of his athletic pants. He slides them down his hips and pushes until they're around his ankles. Without any barriers of clothes in our way, I sink down on his cock the same moment he captures my lips with his. I feel full as his cock settles inside me, deep and exactly where I need him.

"Ride me, baby," he instructs against my lips. His hands move to my hips, helping to guide me up and down his shaft. Our rhythm is choppy, I don't have nearly the stamina that he does, which makes this position hard for me. Although, I do love the way it makes his pubic bone rub my clit with each thrust down as we connect. "That's it, baby, take every inch," he praises as he starts to thrust up.

Our bodies are a sweaty mess as we both chase our orgasms; mine hits me out of nowhere as I spasm around his shaft, making it hard to slide up and down, thanks to the tightness of my convulsing pussy. "I'm fucking coming," he rasps in my ear moments before he slams my body down on his cock so hard, I don't know how he doesn't break me in two.

We both suck in greedy breaths as we hold one another and sink against the couch. The house is still silent, so we successfully got through with our adult time before waking the baby. "Have you thought any more about me knocking you up?" Tristan asks once we've both returned to normal breathing. He brought the idea up last month, but I pushed it off, not really ready to have two under two.

"I'm just not ready. I need some more time and a little larger gap between babies. I promise you that you'll be the first one to know once I'm ready again. I'd like to have my body back for a short amount of time before I give it to someone else," I tell him honestly.

"Whatever you want," he tells me, and I know it is the honest truth.

"I did get you something," I tell him. I'd had plans to give him the envelope after dinner, but the words just kind of slipped out.

"You did?" he asks, a little surprised.

"I did. Well, it is from Olivia and me. I was planning on giving it to you after dinner, but I can do it now," I tell him as I stand up, severing the connection we had. I have to reach for a tissue on the side table quickly, to clean up our mess, since we didn't use a condom.

I find my clothes, tugging them back on while Tristan slips his boxers and T-shirt on, leaving the rest of his clothes on the floor. I find the envelope right where I'd hidden it in plain sight. I walk back over to the couch, taking a seat on his lap once again; this time I'm sideways instead of straddling him.

"This is for you. You don't have to do anything with it if it isn't what you want or are ready for," I say as he takes it from my hands. I hold my breath as he opens the tab and slips the papers out, reading the top bold words *Petition for Adoption*.

His eyes fly to mine and the emotion I see in them has me crying. "How, when?" he asks, the questions tumbling out a jumbled mess.

"I met with Lucy this morning and she had everything ready. She can file it as soon as you sign and return the paperwork. She said after that, it is just a matter of waiting for the courts to put it on a judge's calendar, which she also didn't think would take very long. She's friends with one of the clerks and plans to call in a favor."

"I love you so fucking much," he says as he hugs me tightly. "I need a pen."

I chuckle at his promptness. "I don't have one, but I can go grab one," I tell him just as we hear Olivia start to cry.

"I'll go get her," he insists as we both stand.

My heart melts for the millionth time when I see the two of them as they come out of the bedroom. He's got her in his arms, her head resting on his shoulder as they walk toward me. Olivia's head pops up as she sees me, and she comes alive with excitement. It's as if she knows what just happened; she smacks Tristan's cheeks in that excited baby way, but the sweetest words slip from her lips when she says, "Da-da."

"That's right, baby. I'll be your daddy forever." He kisses her cheek, blowing a raspberry when he's finished, causing her to belly laugh.

We spend the rest of the night, just the three of us. Celebrating what we have, how far we've come, and what's to come for us in the future.

Who would have thought falling for my brother's best friend would have changed my life the way it did, but I'm so glad I walked through fire to get where I'm at. I wouldn't change any of it, as it brought me my daughter and the love of my life.

READY TO HEAD BACK TO SAN FRANCISCO? UP NEXT IS Damien and Trinity. You can pre-order on your favorite platform today!

DID YOU LOVE TRISTAN AND KENDRA? PLEASE CONSIDER leaving a review on your favorite platform.

COMING SOON

Damien
San Francisco Shockwaves Book 4
August 24, 2023
Pre-order on your favorite platform today!
Add on Goodreads today!

ALSO BY SAMANTHA LIND

INDIANAPOLIS EAGLES SERIES

Just Say Yes ~ Scoring The Player

Playing For Keeps ~ Protecting Her Heart

Against The Boards ~ The First Intermission

The Hardest Shot ~ The Game Changer

Rookie Move ~ The Final Period

Box Set 1 {Books 1-3} ~ Box Set 2 {Books 4-6}

Box Set 3 {Books 7-10}

INDIANAPOLIS LIGHTNING SERIES

The Perfect Pitch ~ The Curve Ball

The Screw Ball ~ The Change Up

LYRICS & LOVE SERIES

Marry Me ~ Drunk Girl

Rumor Going 'Round ~ Just A Kiss

STANDALONE TITLES

Tempting Tessa

Until You ~ An Aurora Rose Reynolds Happily Ever Alpha
Crossover Novella

Until Her Smile ~ An Aurora Rose Reynolds Happily Ever
Alpha Crossover Novel

Cocky Doc ~ A Cocky Hero Club Novel

SWEET VALLEY, TENNESSEE

Nothing Bundt Love

Nothing Bundt Forever

SAN FRANCISCO SHOCKWAVES

Ryker

Aiden

Tristan

Damien

ACKNOWLEDGMENTS

I have so many people to thank that I sometimes don't know where to start.

Renee - I seriously couldn't do this without you! It is crazy sometimes how alike we think! Thanks for sticking by my side for so long.

My editing team - Thank you for being so flexible and working with me when I had to step back and put my family first.

My readers! You are the real MVPs here! Thank you for reading my books and loving my characters just as much as I do. Thank you for giving me the grace to step back and make my son the priority while we searched for answers with numerous doctors. After many months, we finally got things solved and he's back to normal! As hard as it was to admit that I needed to step back, I'm so glad that I did, and proud of the story I was able to write to do Tristan and Kendra justice.

xoxo,

Samantha

ABOUT THE AUTHOR

Samantha Lind is a *USA TODAY* Bestselling contemporary romance author. When she's not dreaming up new stories, she can often be found with her family, traveling, reading, watching her boys on the ice or watching her favorite professional team (Go Knights Go!).

Connect with Samantha in the following places:

www.samanthalind.com
samantha@samanthalind.com

Reader Group
Samantha Lind's Alpha Loving Ladies
Good Reads
https://goo.gl/t3R9Vm
Newsletter
https://bit.ly/FDSLNL

facebook.com/SamanthaLindAuthor
twitter.com/samanthalind1
instagram.com/samanthalindauthor
bookbub.com/authors/samantha-lind